Making Amends

by
Melinda Clayton

Making Amends

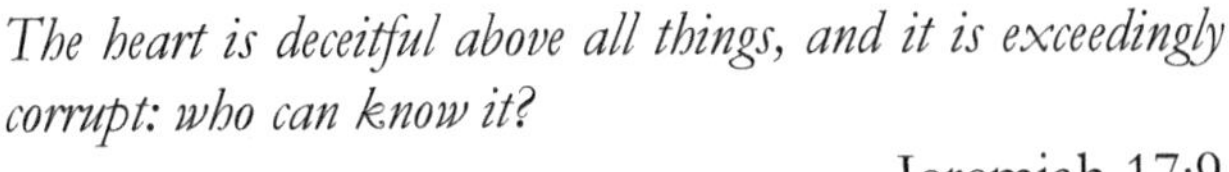

The heart is deceitful above all things, and it is exceedingly corrupt: who can know it?

Jeremiah 17:9

Chapter 1: Tabby

Von's hibiscus plant was dying. I had told her it would, but she's got a stubborn streak a mile wide and she never has liked taking advice from me, especially not when it comes to her plants. For an instant, I couldn't decide whether to tell her about it or let her see it on her own. I have to admit there's something funny about Von when she's angry, the way she pokes her bottom lip out and scrunches up her forehead, looking for all the world like a female version of Elmer Fudd. In the end, though, I decided to tell her. She might *look* funny when she's angry, but being around her when she's angry is no fun at all. If the plant died before she could work her magic on it, I knew I'd come to regret it.

"Von!" I yelled, stepping up into the mobile home that serves as the office for Von's Plants and Such. We had argued over that name, I remembered. "Plants and such? What the hell's that even supposed to mean, Von? What's the *such* part of it?" I had asked, bending over to pick up a stack of seed catalogs that had slipped off the even bigger stack teetering on her kitchen table.

"It's quaint," she'd responded, not even bothering to look up from *Fruiting Plants of Florida*, a book from which she could quote entire paragraphs, and often did. "It's catchy. People will remember it. Just wait and see." She licked her finger and turned the page, letting me know she was finished with the conversation.

As it turned out, she'd been right. Thirty years later, Von's Plants and Such covered nearly three acres and was known for carrying the most healthy, productive plants in central Florida, if not the whole dang state. Von even had an advice column in the *Volusia Sentry*, where she answered everything from, "What're these little shell-looking things all over my Mexican petunias?" (scale bugs) to "Why do my roses keep getting black spot no matter what I do?" (Because you live in Florida, honey.)

For a woman who knew just about everything there was to know about plants in our zone, it was particularly frustrating for her that she couldn't figure out why her hibiscus plants kept dying.

"Von," I repeated, using the doorframe to heft myself up, "we've got to get a step for this door. My knees aren't what they used to be, and one of these days I'm going to get stuck halfway up with no obvious solution but to fall back down, and then I'll have to sue your ass. Anyhow"—I paused to catch my breath—"you're not going to want to hear this, but—"

She shushed me, holding up one calloused hand while with the other she pointed to the little thirteen-inch television perched on the back corner of her desk amid ledgers, receipts, and those endless catalogs. "Tabby," she said, and I knew by the way she said my name something was wrong. Von is not a soft person. When Von goes soft, I go on high alert.

"What?" I moved around the desk so I could see whatever it was she was staring at on the screen. She reached up and pulled me down to sit on an upside-down orange crate, not letting go of my arm once I'd settled.

It was the audio that got my attention before the picture did. "Thirty-year-old Robert Clark," the newscaster was saying, "who was kidnapped by his father at the age of five, was arrested in Tampa, Florida today and charged with the murder of his father, fifty-three-year-old Vernon Clark. According to …"

I couldn't hear any more due to the buzzing in my ears. My eyes wide, I looked at Von, who took my chin in her hand and turned my face back to the screen. There he was, my precious baby, my little boy, the half of my heart that piece-of-shit ex-husband of mine had stolen from me twenty-five years before. Video showed him escorted to a police car, hands behind his back, the officers flanking him, guiding him into the backseat of the cruiser with a hand on top of his head.

Funny, I thought, my last clear thought for a while, they couldn't find him when he disappeared, but let him kill the bastard who stole him and they sure as hell knew how to find him.

Chapter 2: Ricky

"Man, you've got a twin." The slap on the back from Gerry, my coworker, coupled with what he'd said, nearly caused me to drop my coffee. I did have a twin, or at least I *had* a twin, but he had no way of knowing that. I hadn't spoken to anyone about my brother in years, certainly not since accepting a position at *News from the Swamplands*, an independent paper that was unfortunately as cheesy as the name implied.

Setting my Styrofoam cup down before the coffee-sludge spilled down my tie—I only had three, after all, and happened to be wearing my favorite—I scrambled to come up with a response. How could he possibly know about Robert? And what did he know? I hadn't seen my twin brother since my father snatched him off the street a quarter century ago, leaving nothing behind but one of Robert's blue sneakers. Oh, and me. He left me behind, too.

Lucky for me, Gerry is a talker. Before I'd had a chance to come up with any sort of response, he plunged ahead. "Guy arrested for murdering his dad.

Did you see the news this morning? Dude looked *exactly* like you, man. He's in Florida, too. Andy's already on his way to Tampa to cover the story. You sure you aren't adopted? Maybe you guys were separated at birth or something."

Not at birth, but not too long after. We were five years old, Robert and I, that beautiful September afternoon. Our mother met us at the bus stop at the end of the street and walked us home, as she always did. My mother had her share of detractors in those days, people who thought she was an unfit mother, but Robert—Bobby—and I worshipped her.

We didn't care that she was dressed in the same stained t-shirt and baggy sweatpants she'd worn that morning as she'd waved goodbye, following along beside our window until the bus turned the corner. We didn't care that her breath held the permanent odor of spiced rum, the underlying whiff of coffee as she kissed us goodbye having morphed into an intermingled tinge of cola by the end of the day. If our house was unclean—hell, if *we* were unclean—we never noticed; if she slept odd hours it mattered not to us. My mother was a good mother, maybe not by conventional standards, but she was, nonetheless. She still is, because she loves us. There isn't much better than that, is there?

An indescribable feeling started in the pit of my stomach as Gerry rambled on, something like disbelief mixed with hope, both sprinkled with a dose of fear. Gerry paused for breath and I jumped in before he could continue. "What was his name? Did you catch it?" Gerry nodded emphatically before I'd even finished the questions.

"That's the really weird part, bro," he said. "He has the same last name as you. Clark. Crazy, right? Andy's all over it; he wants you to call him as soon as you get to your desk."

I bet he does. If my boss was on his way to Tampa, it wasn't to cover the story of this man's arrest. We were a news organization by the most liberal use of the term, but we didn't focus on stories you could see on CBS, NBC, or ABC. No, we focused on the story *under* the story, as Andy liked to say. Although print circulation of our little rag was miniscule, the online edition had a good-sized following, not just locally but nationally, even, occasionally, internationally.

No one could dig up dirt like *News from the Swamplands.* Andy had a nose for scandal, and he'd learned over the years that society has an insatiable appetite for delving into the dark depths of someone else's despair. The stories didn't have to be about someone famous; I think this is what made Andy's paper so successful. He realized they could be about anyone, so long as the details and secrets were sufficiently horrifying. We'd never be able to compete with publications covering celebrity scandals, but I feel confident saying Andy's take was well into the six-figure range. "Everyone has dirt," he used to say. "It's our job to find it."

It was shameful, really, the way we operated. Our local news might report on a hit-and-run accident, but *Swamplands* went deeper than that. Our job was to dig up whatever we could, not only on the perpetrator, but also on the victim. We didn't report on what happened at the scene, we reported on what happened earlier that day, that year, that lifetime.

An example: Twelve-year-old William Jacobs was

struck and killed by a sport utility vehicle while cross-ing the street on his way to school. The driver of the SUV, forty-four-year-old Todd Matthews, a construc-tion worker from the east side of town, just plain didn't see him. It was early morning, still dark, and William, who was wearing a black hoodie, wasn't in a crosswalk when he was hit. A tragic accident, and that's the way most organizations reported it. But not us.

Further investigation revealed that Matthews, the driver, hadn't been on his way to work as previously assumed. No, he'd been on his way to his girlfriend's house for a little pre-work tête-a-tête. His wife hadn't known that initially, but she certainly did after our front-page report. It wasn't relevant to the story but it sold papers and clicks, and the online comment sec-tion went wild. Comments ranged from, "He's not only a cheat, he's a murderer," to, "He deserves noth-ing short of the death penalty."

Another example: a series of murders in and around Tampa, committed by an unknown intruder dubbed the Silk Stocking Rapist. There were four known victims, all violently sexually assaulted before the intruder strangled three of them to death with a single silk stocking. *Swamplands* mentioned those inci-dents in passing, but the fourth , the lone survivor of the last brutal attack, caught Andy's attention and kept it.

No one had known for certain how the man gained entry to his victims' homes. There was no sign of forced entry in any of the four cases. But when fifty-eight-year-old Thelma Suzette Parker's adult daughter dropped by for an unexpected visit and dis-covered Ms. Parker unconscious on her bedroom floor with a stocking around her neck, a neighbor stepped forward to say she'd seen a white van outside Ms. Parker's home several hours prior, a white van such as might be used by a pest control service. Ms. Parker, transported by ambulance to a local hospital where she remained in intensive care for several weeks, corroborated that information upon awakening from a medically induced coma.

While local news organizations are generally careful about releasing the names of victims of sexual assault, Ms. Parker and her family voluntarily came forward with information in an effort to aid in capturing the assailant. It didn't take much digging for Andy to discover Ms. Parker's history of erotic dancing. Speculation was rampant after that fact became public knowledge. Had a former customer been the attacker? Was it due to a drug deal gone bad? Could it have been a pimp? Were the other victims involved in something seedy, as well?

It hardly mattered that none of the victims had known each other, or that Ms. Parker hadn't danced in nearly twenty years. Nor was there any indication whatsoever she, or any of the victims, had ever dealt in either drugs or prostitution. The click rate skyrocketed, and the comment section exploded. "Lie down with dogs, get up with fleas," was the general theme, once again highlighting the ugly underbelly of online commentary. The assailant vanished without a trace, and a part of me wondered if *Swamplands* was somehow responsible, if we shed so much light in the wrong direction people stopped looking in the right one.

This formula for selling subscriptions wasn't something of which I was proud. I considered my current position as a less-than-savory stepping stone to something better. Paying my dues, was the way I described it to anyone who asked. The fact that I'd been there seven years, three months, thirteen days, and four minutes didn't change my long-term goal, even if it did signify it was harder to reach than I'd previously imagined.

It would only be a matter of time, I knew, before Andy found the current story under the story, and since it happened to be the story of my life, I wasn't looking forward to that moment.

"Guess I'd better get to my desk and make that call," I told Gerry, but it wasn't Andy I needed to call. It was my mother.

Chapter 3: Tabby

I wasn't the best mother; I'll give you that. I mean, it's not as if I could get away with lying about it. I don't know how long the state of Florida keeps records, but I know for a good many years they had stacks and stacks of files on me, so many they had to wheel them into court on a dolly.

I hadn't set out to be a bad mother. Hell, I hadn't set out to be a mother at all. No, what I'd set out to do was get high. Cocaine was my drug of choice in those days, blow, we called it, and it was everywhere, coming in through the southern tip of the peninsula and winding through a network of buyers and sellers until it made its way to me. Or, more accurately, to Vernon Clark, who was only too happy to share. That sorry bastard has—*had*, I suppose I should say, given the morning news—no end of ways to try to wreck my sorry life.

Let me tell you, one sure-fire way to catch the attention of Florida authorities is to show up at the hospital half dead of an overdose and fourteen weeks pregnant with twins. Even more shocking than waking up in a hospital bed was the barrage of angry questions from the doctor.

"When was your last period?"

"What?"

"Your period. When did you last have it?"

I blinked up at him, trying to figure out where I was and who he was. Why was this angry man asking me about my period, and what business was it of his? Besides, I had no idea what the answer might be. It could have been days, weeks, or months. Hell, for all I knew, I was on it at that moment. My days weren't cut up into the usual twenty-four hour stretches of time.

Vernon and I existed in a haze, either using blow or scheming ways to get it. During our most desperate times we'd set up along the off ramps from I-4, holding up signs saying *Homeless and Hungry* or some such thing. It wasn't a lie, exactly. We *were* homeless and hungry, wandering from binge to binge, crashing on floors and couches in the nastiest of places, sometimes hiding under bushes and park benches when that was the only option. But we didn't want the money for food, no siree; we needed it to avoid the comedown. An addict will do just about anything to dodge the crash.

Besides, we were used to being homeless. By the time I was put out on the street at eighteen I'd spent time in nine different foster homes and done a stint at the Baptist Children's Home, which is where I met Vernon. Maybe it was inevitable that in the early hours of that dark March morning, I'd once again caught the attention of the Florida Department of Health and Rehabilitative Services, only this time from the opposite end. I'd gone from victim to perpetrator, abused to abuser.

"You're pregnant," the doctor enunciated, the syllables harsh and exaggerated. "I'll ask you one more time. When was your last period?"

I shook my head and shrugged, not meaning to be disrespectful, but too ashamed to admit I'd had no inkling, no awareness of physical changes, no memory of … well, of much of anything for quite a stretch of time.

The look of disgust on the doctor's face was unmistakable, but to his credit all he said was, "We'll need an ultrasound," before turning to bark orders at someone outside my line of vision.

The next few hours were a blur, but two phrases ring clear as a bell through my memory: *there are two of them*, and *call the Department*. It took a minute for the *there are two of them* part to sink in, but the *call the Department* one took hold immediately.

I was a young, lost, foolish junkie, a bag bitch, as Vernon called me whenever I rejected his advances. But one thing I did know, maybe the only thing I knew, was that I did not want my babies taken care of by the Florida Department of Health and Rehabilitative Services. I knew an argument could be made that they'd saved me from a childhood of abuse and neglect, but there are different degrees to the word *saved*. If you've ever been caught up in the system, you'll know what I mean.

I vowed then and there no matter what it took or how painful it got, I'd get clean. And I'm proud to say, even with Vernon's constant badgering and temptations, even with social workers all around me watching my every move, even with the paralyzing fear of prenatal damage hanging over me, I was clean when I delivered my beautiful boys.

Now, the years afterward … well, that's a different story.

Chapter 4: Von

Breathe," I told Tabby, giving her arm a shake. The news segment had ended a good thirty seconds ago, but Tabby still sat with her eyes glued to the screen, mouth hanging open in apparent shock. "Breathe," I told her again, and yanked her arm harder. To my relief, I heard a sharp intake of breath and saw her shoulders rise.

"Bobby," she said, and when she turned to me I saw, for just a second, the skinny, shaking girl who'd stood up in a room of crusty older folks and, after a couple of stumbles, managed to say, "Hi. My name is Tabby. Tabatha. My name is Tabatha Clark, and Lord knows, I need some help."

That girl had been terrified, but I knew the quivering wasn't all fear. She was a mess. Cocaine, I could see, and it hadn't been kind to her. Her hair was of the dirty-blond shade that's almost no shade at all, and she had it pulled back so tight the outward corners of her eyes were tilted up, making her face look not only thin, but alien. She had the telltale runny nose of a hardcore user, and when she raised her hand to swipe at the discharge with a wadded tissue, I saw angry claw marks up and down the bony arm. Looking closer, I could see the hems of her sleeves were stained a dark red, the color barely noticeable against the cheap plaid fabric. Snow bugs, then, that god-awful feeling of bugs crawling around under the skin. This girl had it bad. I only hoped she wasn't so burned out she couldn't recover.

In contrast, the middle-aged woman beside her had been plump and polished, permed hair perfectly sprayed, makeup thick enough to scrape off with a squeegee. Dressed in a conservative navy-blue skirt and jacket, she stood out like a ... well, like what she was: a social worker interrupting a recovery meeting. I must admit, I was none too pleased by her presence, and given the shuffling and muttering noises around me, I could tell my Friday night playmates were just as displeased.

We never did a tally, but I'm fairly confident saying the majority of us had at one time or another been involved with the system. Social worker, probation officer, counselor—it didn't matter which system representative was there. Though they meant well, it was an encroachment, not only of our privacy, but also of our recovery. Honesty is crucial to recovery, but our honesty often contained tidbits of information we'd prefer our various system representatives not to have. It wasn't their fault, really, but their reports sometimes caused more damage than they helped contain. The social worker hanging on to our latest member was met with suspicion, at best. What the hell was she doing there, anyway?

Before any of us could ask, she leaned toward the

girl to whisper something in her ear. The girl—
Tabatha Clark, she'd said—nodded, and with a quick
pat on Tabatha's arm, the woman turned to leave,
heels clicking on the old wooden floor of our borrowed church before she went out the heavy swinging
doors with a *swoosh*. That took care of that problem,
anyway.

It was clear Tabatha Clark had more to say, so we
waited. We had nowhere else to be, at least nowhere
else we *should* be. We were, by and large, a patient
bunch, after all we'd been through, and it was plain to
see this girl was in trouble.

"Well," she said, finally. "I guess y'all know why
I'm here." She had a soft voice with a slight southern
drawl. I wondered if she was a native to Florida, maybe from the panhandle, somewhere a little farther
north than our central Florida locale, judging by the
hint of accent. "I don't know how much I'm supposed to say," she continued. "Am I supposed to tell
y'all what all I've done?"

"Just tell us whatever you feel comfortable telling
us," said Bob. Bob Linwood was our chairperson,
twenty years sober at that time, but dead of a heart
attack in '96. Alcohol had been Bob's demon, but it
was lysergic acid diethylamide, LSD, that caused the
real damage. "One time," he'd told us several times,
as if he couldn't quite believe it. "That's all it took."
According to Bob, that one time had resulted in a trip
so horrifying he'd attempted to gouge his own eyes
out to escape the hallucinations. "Demons," he'd told
us. "That's the only way I can describe them. I'd rather be blind than ever have to see them again." LSD
is a wicked, wicked drug.

The gentle light of the chandeliers reflected off his dark glasses as he turned his face in the general direction of Tabatha's voice and waited.

"The biggest thing is, I'm pregnant," she said, right before she swooned. I was the closest one to her, so it was up to me to hop a pew and catch her before she fell.

But that was all a long, long time ago, and sitting in my trailer office, seeing the ghost of twenty-one-year-old Tabby flitter across fifty-one-year-old Tabby's face, I knew no matter how difficult it got, she'd be able to handle it. Tabby always was a survivor. And, hell, if she fell, I'd still be there to catch her. In the thirty years since that first swoon we'd become much more than sponsor and sponsored. We'd become the closest of friends, more like sisters, really.

Before I could say anything, the sound of crickets filled the office. That was Tabby's little joke, her ringtone for Ricky, the twin she still had. No amount of contact with him was ever enough; I think she was afraid even at the age of thirty he might disappear just as his brother had twenty-five years before. "I tried to call you and what did I get?" she'd ask Ricky, frustrated he hadn't picked up in time. "Crickets. Nothing but crickets."

"Thank God," she said now, digging in her pocket for the phone. As she spoke to Ricky I shuffled the receipts and reports on my desk into slightly more organized chaos, then grabbed the broom to sweep the inevitable sugar sand out the door, though I knew my efforts were pointless. Ted McGillis, my third-in-command, was better at bringing dirt in than getting dirt out, and with Tabby in Tampa, where I felt sure she was headed, he'd have to take over her inventory duties.

As for me, I was torn, as I so often am these days. I wanted to accompany Tabby but couldn't possibly leave my husband for such an extended length of time. Ben had good days and bad days, the Alzheimer's (we called it Old Timer's) waxing and waning just enough to give us false hope. He still came to the nursery with me, but on his bad days Ted and I spent more time tending to him than we did to the plants. I wasn't close enough to my other employees to entrust either my husband or my nursery to them, and I couldn't leave Ted to deal with everything alone.

Tabby ended the call with her son right as I put the broom away. "Ricky's on his way to the house," she said. "He's taking me to Tampa."

"Tabby—"

"Hush, Von. I know you'd go if you could."

I nodded. Of course she knew, but I still felt as if I were letting her down. After all, in some ways I'd known Bobby since before he was born. Tabby used to talk to those unborn babies all the time, rubbing her stomach while she did, even calling them by name. When I'd point out she couldn't possibly know which was which, she'd insist that she did. Maybe she did, who am I to say? Sometimes I thought Tabby had a sort of sixth sense, as they call it. Whether she did or didn't, one thing's for certain: She was always overly protective of Bobby. It was almost as if she knew her time with him was limited; she just didn't know yet who the limiter would be.

Losing him nearly killed her, but it saved her, too, in an odd way. That was something I never expressed to her, but it's true, just the same.

"At least come get a quick bite to eat before you go," I said, putting a fresh liner in the garbage can. "I'll go fetch Ben and let Ted know he's in charge for the rest of the day."

"I can't wait, Von, you know I can't." Her face was flushed, her eyes bright. I couldn't help but wonder what thoughts were buzzing through her head at that moment. How would I feel if, after twenty-five years of searching, I'd just seen my missing son arrested for the murder of his father? I couldn't even begin to imagine.

"I'm not hungry, anyway," Tabby continued, standing to leave, tripping over the orange crate in her haste. "Tell you what—damned crate—why don't you come to my place and set out some sandwich stuff while I pack? We'll eat on the road."

I smiled at her use of "my place." We shared a duplex, had for more years than I could count. Her place and my place were dang near the same thing.

"All right, but go ahead and get a head start. I have to round up Ben, and this isn't one of his better days."

"Sounds good. Poor Ben." She hesitated. "Von, if you take too long ..."

"If I take too long go ahead and go. I know you have to. If that happens, call me and let me know you got there okay."

"I will." She grabbed her purse out of the bottom desk drawer as I maneuvered the drop from the trailer door to go find Ben. Tabby was right; I needed to invest in a step. My knees had twelve years on hers, and they were starting to rebel.

Chapter 5: Von

I found Ben standing among the sago palms, hands on his hips and muttering. "Veronica, what the hell were you thinking?" he asked as soon as he saw me. Although it was only ten in the morning, the bill of his hat was soaked through with sweat and the plaid flannel shirt he'd insisted on wearing was stuck to his chest. I'd known better than to let him wear it, but I was no match for Ben's stubborn side. I'd held onto the hope that, like our daughter when she was young, he'd eventually calm down enough from the tantrum to come to the realization on his own that it had been a bad idea. And it had. If May was any indication, summer was going to be long, hot, and unbearably humid. Even the sand was hot, burning through the thin soles of my sneakers.

"Honey, let's go have some lunch." I spoke quietly, calmly, as I'd learned to do when he was agitated. I reached for his arm, but he yanked it away. One of the hardest parts of having a loved one taken by Alzheimer's, I'd come to understand, was learning to deal with the anger—anger that was more often than not directed at me, more often than not for something I hadn't done.

"How the hell am I supposed to mow with all these damn bushes in the way?"

I knew immediately what he was thinking and it made sense, particularly for a mind that lived more in the past than the present. When Ben and I first married the nursery was our yard, except that it wasn't a nursery back then, it was an overgrown horse pasture that had belonged to my maternal grandparents, then to my mother, and finally to me. When my mother passed on, the first thing I did was sell the horses. I was in no shape to care for them and I needed the money. I was in recovery by then, but I'd spent my late teens and early twenties making a mess of things. I was working hard to make amends (step nine), and paying back the people I'd stolen from was one of those amends.

When Ben and I married he moved in with me, into the little trailer that had been my mother's and now serves as the office of Von's Plants and Such. Ben had worked for a local landscaping company; that's how I met him. Something was growing all over that pastureland and I had no idea what it was. I finally yanked up a plant with the thought of taking it to Ace Hardware or somewhere to ask if anyone knew what it was and how I could get rid of it.

At a four-way stop on the way into town I ended up behind a rattling, belching landscape truck. One glance at that fine man's reflection in his side-view mirror and I decided then and there it'd be a whole lot more fun to ask *him*, so I put the car in park, grabbed the plant out of the passenger floorboard and ran up to his window, all the while ignoring the honking car behind me.

Dogfennel, it turns out. That night, over a dinner of fried mullet and cabbage at the diner outside of town, he offered to help me get rid of it. He offered a few other things, too, but I'm not going to go into all that, given it was of a more personal nature.

Between the two of us we had that land looking better than it ever had during my lifetime. The rotted fences were dug up, the bahiagrass was mown and overseeded, and although I thought the day would never come, the dogfennel was finally eradicated. It was during that time I discovered I loved working outside, loved working with plants. The smell of the soil, the greenery and juices … It was clean, if that makes sense. It was honest. A long, long way from the dirty time I spent on the streets.

Not long after I met Tabby—right around the time our girl Martha was set to start kindergarten—Ben and I started talking about turning that old horse pasture into a fulltime nursery. We figured our old trailer would make a decent office, and Ben already had a lot of the equipment we'd need. We sold off a couple of acres and started looking closer to town for a little fixer-upper we could turn into a home.

We both agreed we didn't want to live on the job, so to speak. When you live on the job, you're never *off* the job. Besides, I thought it'd be nice for Martha to be closer to friends. I pictured her in a group of girls, riding bikes along the sidewalk, and knew we were making the right decision. When I was a little girl, I'd hated living so far out of town. I'd missed out on all the important things, all the things the other kids could walk to, like Jenna Lou's sixth birthday party, or readying the senior float for the Christmas parade. I didn't want Martha to grow up as resentful as I had.

We used to spend Sunday afternoons driving around town, looking at *For Sale* signs and writing down realtor names and numbers. It was on one of those drives we came across the little duplex. The price was right and the more we thought about it, the more sense it made. We could live in one side and rent out the other for extra income. I worried a little bit about having strangers right next door, but as it turned out that was wasted worry. Tabby is the only renter we've ever had.

Now here was Ben, right when I was trying to hurry home for Tabby, reliving the past and frustrated with me for putting plants in the way of his mower. "It's okay, honey," I said, reaching for him again. "We'll sell these. They won't be in your way, I promise. Now let's go find some air conditioning and eat some lunch."

He came with me, still frowning and, I could tell, still confused. Ben had always been a handsome man, maybe even more so at seventy. He was tall and trim and even after all our years together, I still caught myself watching him sometimes, blushing at the thoughts in my own head. He swiped a sleeve across his sweaty forehead and looked down at me. "We don't live here anymore," he said quietly, his eyes searching mine.

"No, baby, we don't," I confirmed around the lump in my throat. "We live in the duplex, with Tabby." It was so unfair, so damned unfair, after all we'd been through and all we'd overcome, for this good man to have been reduced to this. For our *marriage* to have been reduced to this.

"Vonny," he said, stroking my cheek with the back of a callused hand. "Don't cry, Von. I was just a little confused. I'm at the nursery on a Wednesday morning. It's May, hotter than hell, and I don't know what I was thinking, wearing this shirt. I'll change it at home. But"—he stopped and looked at me—"why, exactly, are we going home now? It's not time for lunch, is it?" He consulted his watch. "What's happened? Is it Martha?"

Our daughter, married with two teenagers, had lived just outside of Tampa in a little community called Ruskin for years. Suddenly I couldn't believe I hadn't thought of it sooner. Martha was a clerical worker at the Hillsborough County Sheriff's Office. Bobby had been arrested in Tampa by the city police department, but I wondered if Martha, as a county employee, might be able to find any information that could help Tabby. I'd call her as soon as I got Ben settled at home.

I wanted to share Tabby's news with Ben, but I wasn't sure how much he'd understand. "Do you remember Bobby?" I asked, and he shot me an irritated look.

"Of course I remember Bobby. Why wouldn't I?"

I ignored the question and plunged ahead. "Well, he's been found," I said. "Maybe not under the best of circumstances, but he's been found and Tabby's going to go see him, or at least try to. I don't know if they'll let her. Wouldn't it be awful, after all this time, if they don't let her see him?" I knew I wasn't making much sense, but the overwhelming truth of the circumstances was finally sinking in.

"Found?" Ben asked. "Woman, what're you talking about? Who won't let her see him? He went by on his tricycle, not five minutes ago, with Ricky standing on the back like they always do. I keep telling Tabby one of these days they're going to flip that thing over and someone's going to get hurt." He gave me a knowing look. "If Tabby'd lay off the booze, she wouldn't keep losing him."

Truer words were never spoken, even if they were spoken twenty-five years too late.

Chapter 6: Ricky

If all was well on I-4, my mother's home was about a half hour trip from my office. I took my time getting there, which may seem strange. I suppose I was trying to hold onto the last moments of life as I knew it. I had no idea what would happen once we made contact with Bobby, other than that things would never be the same.

I was also, on some level, trying to work through a tangle of confused emotions. I had very few memories of my brother, and most of those were vague feelings and impressions rather than clear-cut memories. I remembered a breezy summer day at the beach, the vague dizziness I always felt from sun glinting off sand and water, the numbing sound of the waves, the distant voice of my mother. *Look, boys, a dolphin! Two of them. Do you see?* I remember her standing no more than ankle deep, dressed in a purple two-piece bathing suit that made her look odd to me. My mother wore jeans and t-shirts. The woman pointing out to sea, long hair blowing in the wind, dark sunglasses hiding her eyes, I found slightly alarming if only because of her unfamiliarity.

I followed the line of her index finger but could see nothing other than the meshing of sky and waves, interrupted only by a squadron of pelicans diving for fish. Nevertheless, I nodded. I didn't want to disappoint this happy sounding lady in the purple bathing suit. She stood for a moment longer before trudging back up the beach to sit under an umbrella with Aunt Von, and I turned back to the hole I'd been digging with my brother.

Our goal, I remember (although I'm certain we didn't define it as such) was to dig a hole deep enough to create our own swimming hole. Our mother was terrified of sharks (*See all those birds, boys? That means there are fish, and where there are fish, there are sharks*); consequently, we were only allowed to play at the very edge of the water where the waves run out of steam and sluice up onto the sand.

I don't know how old we were, maybe three or four. Definitely no older than five, since that's when the world as we'd known it ended. I remember enjoying my brother that day, aside from the occasional not-so-accidental scoop of sand in the face. And I remember the sound of his laughter, bubbling into the wind every time an incoming wave collapsed the walls of our little hole and forced us to start over. I laughed with him; how could I not?

Bobby was the more adventurous twin, or so I've heard all my life. Born a minute and fifty-three seconds after him, I was apparently destined from birth to be the follower. According to Uncle Ben, Bobby liked to lead me into trouble.

I always enjoyed hearing Uncle Ben's stories about

Bobby because unlike my mother and Aunt Von, he shied away from creating the image of an angel-child in favor of remembering Bobby as he was, a tenacious, strong-willed little boy, at least according to Uncle Ben. When the shadow of Bobby's absence became too much to bear, when I knew no matter what I did or how well I did it I'd never be able to compete with the memory of a different five-year-old boy, I'd go to Uncle Ben and he'd set me straight.

"Ricky," he'd say. "Bobby wasn't a saint; he was a boy. It's like with dead people. Now, don't look at me that way. I don't mean Bobby *is* a dead person. I mean it's *like* with a dead person. Folks always make them into saints. My grandmomma, God rest her soul, was the meanest woman ever to walk this earth. My uncle used to say Grandmomma was so mean all she had to do was walk by the churn to turn sweet milk into buttermilk. But as soon as that woman kicked the bucket, you'd have thought she was the next best thing to Mother Mary, given what folks said at the funeral.

"Your momma, God bless her, has grieved so hard and missed Bobby so much she only remembers the good. That's all right, if that's how she needs to handle it. But you don't need to be trying to compete with a ghost. Your momma might not remember it, but I do. Bobby spent a good part of his time with us in the time-out corner, and he earned more swats on the behind than any child that young has a right to earn. He tested your momma; he tested everyone. He was a funny little cuss, stubborn as a mule. Smart as a whip, too. But he wasn't a saint, and don't you go believing he was."

My clearest memory of Bobby, which is ironically

the one I've spent my life trying to forget, is of him being snatched right off the sidewalk in front of me, yanked up into the cab of the truck and just … gone.

I tapped the brake and turned right onto my mother's street, slowly cruising toward the duplex and the spot from which Bobby was taken. The bougainvillea wasn't in bloom as it had been that fall, but the fire hydrant was still there. The September afternoon my brother had been taken we'd been playing hide-and-seek. *Three, two, one, ready or not, here I come!* The bougainvillea, brilliant red, hung wild over the fence of the neighbor behind us, creating a canopy of sorts and providing a perfect hiding spot along the sidewalk if one was careful of the thorns. I'd been hiding; Bobby had been seeking, until the game had flipped and we'd spent the following twenty-five years seeking Bobby.

In the beginning, friends and neighbors tried to talk my mother into moving. "It'll be too painful," they said, "too much of a reminder. Start fresh, find a new house and start over with Ricky." But my mother insisted on staying, hoping, I think, that one day Bobby would find his way back to us. Had I been allowed a voice, I'd have voted to move. I spent the rest of my childhood trying to avoid that spot. I wasn't afraid I'd also be taken. No, it was more complicated than that. I missed my brother, or at least I assume I did, but in the back of my mind a troubling thought settled and grew roots: why did my father want my brother, but not me?

A part of me wonders if my childhood would have been different, if maybe I wouldn't have developed this anxious, self-defeating personality if I hadn't had to look at that spot every damn day. Another part of me can't imagine having lived anywhere but next to Aunt Von and Uncle Ben. I remember once, I must have been in first or second grade, when we had to draw a family tree. It was literally in the shape of a tree, with family members added on as branches.

Mine was pitiably small, consisting of my mother, me, and Aunt Von and Uncle Ben. In a burst of creativity I also drew Bobby. I didn't want to leave him out, but I wasn't sure if missing relatives counted so I drew him superimposed on me. I did not draw my father. I was no longer allowed to mention him; he'd ceased to exist in my life, at least publicly. My own private recriminations and doubts were another issue entirely.

Proud of my efforts, I handed the assignment in to Mrs. Cross. *Older than dirt*, is how my mother once described Mrs. Cross to Aunt Von. *And her name fits her to a "T."* I hadn't known what my mother meant by that, but I did know I was a little afraid of Mrs. Cross, who had a tendency to blur the line between stern and just plain hurtful, as she did that particular day.

"Richard," she said, slapping the paper down onto my desk, "redo this. This branch is a mess; you traced over it so much it looks like two people instead of one. And those people are not a part of your family. They're *black*, boy, are you blind?"

I guess I had been, because I can honestly say until that moment I'd never taken so much as a second to consider what color Aunt Von and Uncle Ben might be. In the absence of blood relatives we had a tendency to collect relatives based on love. Aunt Von and Uncle Ben *were* my relatives; I didn't care what Mrs. Cross said.

Luckily, my family agreed. "Take a zero, Ricky, 'cause you ain't doing this assignment over again," my mother said. "She wanted a family tree; she got a family tree." Aunt Von put her hands on either side of my face and kissed me on the forehead, a much more generous show of affection than she usually displayed.

Lost in thought, I swung into the driveway and nearly ran over my mother. Before I could stop she had her hand on the door handle, ready to hop in. Uncle Ben, wearing a ridiculously heavy flannel shirt for such a hot day, rounded the car to put my mother's bag in the trunk, then stopped by my window.

"Remember, Ricky, he wasn't a saint. He was just a boy. It's like with dead people." He looked hard at me. "You understand what I'm saying?" I did, and screw Mrs. Cross, I thought for easily the hundredth time over the years. This man is my uncle—my father, really—failing memory, silly flannel shirt, and all.

Chapter 7: Tabby

Ricky didn't seem to want to talk, and, rightly or wrongly, I was grateful for that. My mind was swimming, or maybe it was drowning. I had too many thoughts to collect, and the pounding of my heart only added to the confusion. I felt as if I must either suffer a heart attack or faint; surely, a heart couldn't race like that forever.

I glanced at Ricky, knowing he must be feeling some of the same. Such a good boy, my Ricky. Never complained, never talked back, always did as he was told, always tried to be a good enough child to fill the space of two.

Or maybe not; maybe that's my own interpretation of his behaviors. Ricky had always kept to himself; I'd never really known what he was thinking. At birth he'd been too weak and underweight to make a fuss. Oh, yes, the blow had done some damage. Not too much for us to handle, thank God, but some.

I'd spent the majority of my pregnancy being prepared for the possibility my babies would be severely disabled. Now they say the early studies exaggerated things, but who wants to take that risk? You'd be crazy to take a chance like that. Back then, I was told at best the babies would face mental challenges; at worst, they'd face physical ones, too.

Both boys were underweight at birth. I don't remember what their scores were on that test—what's it called?—the Apgar. But I remember the doctor saying they were sluggish. By that first evening, whatever sluggishness Bobby had felt was long gone. That baby was screaming his lungs out, fists all balled up and face purple. Ricky, on the other hand, was sleeping, though I can't imagine how.

That pattern continued over the precious few years I had with both of them. Bobby was the rambunctious one, the one always wearing me out. Ricky, bless his heart, waited his turn without complaining. Did I sometimes neglect Ricky in order to tend to Bobby? Possibly. Probably. But at the time I felt I had no choice. Ask any mother who she'll respond to quickest, the screaming baby or the quiet one, and you'll have your answer.

Did that hurt Ricky? That was one of the hundreds of questions that kept me awake in the early morning hours. Someone once told me three o'clock in the morning was the haunting hour. If that's true—and I believe it is—it's only us haunting ourselves. No one can torture us more than we can torture ourselves, because we know all the bruises to push and cuts to salt and we do a mighty fine job of pushing and salting. The early morning hours between three and six are always the worst because the world is too quiet for us to find a distraction; it's all laid bare. Whatever you've done, whatever you can be blamed for, stares you smack in the face. You have no choice but to admit it.

But admitting it doesn't make it go away; that's the crux of it all. Wake up to go pee in the wee hours of the morning and the accusations are right back at it, tearing away at you as if you'd never acknowledged them to begin with.

It's an exhausting way to live, I'll tell you that. Imagine it: Every single day of your life, you start out a loser. Not just a loser, but a loser who, due to your own poor decisions, pulls other people down with you—and not just other people, but your own children. Your own flesh and blood. Imagine knowing the mistakes you made before they even existed will cause them problems their entire lives.

It doesn't matter whether or not it's scientifically true, because it's what you *believe*. That's all that matters.

One thought that keeps buzzing through my head is a new one, but it takes its place right alongside all the old ones that have dogged me so long.

They knew his name. *Thirty-year-old Robert Clark, who was kidnapped by his father at the age of five, was arrested in Tampa, Florida today …*

No doubt they'd looked into his background before it hit the airwaves, although these days, that's hardly a given, but how can it be that he was right there all along, only two hours away, and no one ever found him? I'd told myself over the years they must have changed names, moved far away, maybe even left the country, but what if that wasn't true? Vernon no doubt kept him from me when he was little, but Bobby was thirty years old this past January. He'd had a good dozen years to find me on his own. Hell, I was in the same place I'd always been, waiting for him to come home. So why hadn't he?

I held no illusions. I could list plenty of reasons he might have chosen to stay away from me, but why didn't he at least try to find Ricky? That just didn't make sense to me.

Chapter 8: Von

By the time I finally managed to get Ben settled down I figured Tabby and Ricky must have been halfway to Tampa. It wasn't that Ben was being difficult; it was the opposite, in fact. He'd gone back in time again, this time to sweltering summer days when we were young and a midday break meant something other than seeing my best friend drive off to visit her missing son who'd just been charged with murdering his father.

We hadn't been able to get enough of each other back then, and seeing Ben's leer, I nearly laughed in spite of the anxiety I felt for Tabby. I'd barely waved Tabby down the road when I turned to see him unbuckling his belt, the randy old coot. "It's just you and me now, toots," he said, and I did laugh, then. It was an old line, one that conjured up memories of entangled limbs and young sweaty bodies, and I wasn't sure which was more amusing, the mental comparison I did between my previous young, sweaty body and the current one I inhabited, or the sight of

Ben battling both his arthritic feet and bum back in an attempt to strip off his pants.

"Woman, what's got into you?" he asked, propping against the doorframe, caught somewhere between a bend and a crouch, one foot weakly flailing at the pant leg he couldn't dislodge. This only served to make me laugh harder, and I'm ashamed to say the slightly insulted expression on his face did nothing to sober me.

"I'm just happy," I told him, and it wasn't exactly a lie. I was sad almost beyond bearing at the latest blow life had dealt Ben and me and worried nearly sick about what Tabby and Ricky might find in Tampa, but I loved my husband through and beyond anything this world could throw at us, and that made me happy. He rewarded my answer with a smile, one of those Ben smiles that transformed his whole face into an almost textbook smiley-face, his eyes tilted up at the outward corners, the wrinkles and grooves of his later years only highlighting the effect. Lord, I thought for the millionth time in my life, I have married one fine man.

As it always did, the reality of the moment settled in, pressing down my shoulders and weighing on my heart. I would have to manipulate my husband, I knew, as I did more and more frequently as his illness took hold. It pained me to do so; Ben and I had always had an honest relationship, a rarity in this world, if I do say so myself. But when an ill spouse spends so much time in a make-believe world, sometimes the only choice the survivor has is to join in that world and pretend right along with him.

"Tell you what, baby," I said, coming to stand in front of him, circling my arms around his waist and leaning my head against his chest. "You go warm up the bed for me, and I'll go freshen up for you." He laughed, pulling me close.

"You're fresh enough for me exactly the way you are," he said, and I wanted to cry, because I knew he meant it. How many lunch breaks had we spent doing what he wanted now? Hundreds? Thousands? Smelling of earth and plants and sweat, and loving every second of it for the honesty it represented.

But I had come to know my husband's illness, the unpredictability of it. The last time Ben had propositioned me in the middle of the day he'd forgotten what he was about in the middle of removing his clothes. He went from unbuttoning to buttoning, cursing because he couldn't figure out how to get the belt back through the loops. The time before he'd looked up and not known me. After all, in Ben's mind at that moment we were young and beautiful. In reality, I'm a sixty-three-year-old woman—a sixty-three-year-old woman in fantastic shape, if I do say so myself, but when you think you're bedding a twenty-five-year-old and you look up and see someone who looks like her mother, well … He didn't say anything. He didn't have to; his face said it all. So I had learned to protect myself.

I stood on my toes and kissed his neck in the soft spot right under his chin, my favorite spot in all the world. "I know you mean that," I said, "but let me freshen up a little, anyway. I've got something special planned."

He rewarded me with a laugh deep in his throat; I felt the rumble against my cheek. "Well, then, Momma, hurry up and don't keep me waiting."

"I won't," I promised, and kissed him full on the mouth to seal the deal, knowing all the while the seal wasn't valid. I walked him to the bedroom, helped him pull down the covers, kissed him again as he climbed under them, and winked at him through tears as I closed the door. He'd be asleep before I even managed to dial Martha. I let myself cry just for a second before I picked up the phone and scrolled to her number. I figured Ben and I deserved at least that.

Chapter 9: Ricky

You won't be able to see him today, Aunt Tabby."

We'd been half an hour outside of Tampa when Martha called my mother on her cell. Mom put the phone on speaker and held it between us as I maneuvered my way through lunchtime traffic on I-4. "I missed the news this morning, but Mom filled me in. Why don't you head over to our house? Stay with us until you get this all sorted out."

I glanced over at Mom, afraid to take my eyes off the road for too long. Every resident thinks their state holds the title of World's Worst Drivers, but Florida really does; I'd bet money on it. "Florida cars don't come equipped with blinkers" was one of Uncle Ben's favorite sayings, and by all indications, it was true. "These damn drivers are crazy as hell" was another of his maxims, one no doubt truer than the first.

Anyway, as quick as my glance was, I could still see the impatience etched on Mom's face. She didn't want to go to Martha's house or anywhere else until she'd seen Bobby, and I said as much, prompting Martha's unwelcome reply.

"What do you mean we can't see him today?" Mom's voice bordered on shrill and I dared to take one hand off the wheel to give her a quick pat on the knee. Honestly, I didn't know what to expect of my mother in such stressful circumstances. I knew of her history of drug and alcohol abuse, obviously, but I truly didn't have any direct memories of that time, at least none I felt had harmed me in any way. Sure, I remember her breath smelling funny, and I remember her falling into fits of giggles when she sometimes stumbled. I remember her sleeping a great deal in the afternoons, but Bobby and I didn't care. If anything, we took advantage of her unconscious state, stealing sweets or staying up past our bedtime to watch grownup shows we weren't allowed to watch.

Still, I knew how serious she was about sobriety and I couldn't imagine a more taxing situation than the one we were in. I was more than a little anxious myself, and found myself working overtime to try to soothe my mother's tattered emotions.

"Of course we can see him; we've been looking for him for decades. What the hell are you talking about, Martha? And what about bail? We can pay it. I have some money saved back. He'll come home with me until the trial." My calming pat on her knee had obviously not had the intended effect.

"That's not how it works," Martha said. "This will be a non-bondable case. He's charged with first degree murder; he'll be brought before the magistrate." She paused. "I know it's hard, Aunt Tabby." Her voice was calm, patient, just as it had been throughout my childhood. Six years our senior, Martha was often saddled with keeping an eye on Bobby and me. She never seemed to particularly mind the role, and I adored her. Have been half in love with her all my life, to tell the truth. Bobby loved her, too, although it might not have always been obvious. He took a great deal of pleasure in trying to rattle her, I think precisely because he couldn't, not even the time he scaled the rose trellis and ended up lying on his belly, grinning at us from the roof of the shed.

I remember standing next to Martha, torn between fear for my brother's safety and envy because he was so much braver than I. Martha, though, she just stood with her hands on her hips, head cocked to the side, looking exactly like a ten-year-old version of Aunt Von. Finally she looked at me and said, "Come on, Ricky, let's go get some ice cream. Momma's almost out, but there should be plenty for the two of us." She took me by the hand and pulled me around the corner then stopped, pressing a finger to her lips with a grin.

The noise was terrible—a scrabbling, clawing, tearing noise, followed by a thud. Then Bobby was beside me, knees and elbows scraped, blood dripping down his forehead as he plucked a good-sized splinter out of the pad of one index finger. "So," he said, "what flavor is it? I hope it ain't vanilla because I really want me some chocolate."

My mother's voice, edging on hysteria, pulled me from my memories. "I don't need permission to see my own son! Don't you know how long I've waited? They can't make me wait even longer." I reached to pat her again.

"I know, Aunt Tabby, it's crazy. And it would be different if he were still a missing minor, but as it is there are procedures they have to follow. Come to our house and we'll make some phone calls, okay? I have a friend who works at the police department, a woman in my book club. She'll help walk us through whatever we need to do."

Mom didn't answer for a few seconds and I looked over to see her crying, the back of her hand pressed hard against her mouth as if holding in the sounds of her distress would make it disappear.

"We'll be there within the hour, Martha," I answered for my mother. "Thank you."

"We'll get this sorted out, Ricky." Her voice had softened. "She'll get to see him, but maybe not today."

We signed off and for the remainder of the drive to Martha's house the car was silent, other than the sound of my mother's crying.

Chapter 10: Tabby

The setting was beautiful, a west-facing sunporch overlooking a lake that had probably been constructed as a retention pond but was doing a damn fine job hiding that fact. Palms stretched towards the blue sky, their fronds rustling in the afternoon breeze, and Sandhill Cranes high-stepped along the bank in search of a snack. Dragonflies flitted across the lawn, occasionally bumping into the screen with a lazy buzz. Had I been at Martha's house for any other reason, I'd have relaxed, tilted my head back against the Adirondack chair, and ignored that ever-present urge for a drink, something fancy, with a tiny umbrella and sweat drops dripping down the side. As it was, I sat stiff as a board, unable to relax, but still craving that drink, umbrella or no.

It's true what they say, or at least it has been for me: The cravings never really go away. Certain situations, sights, smells, times, and I feel the craving like a deep itch. In the beginning that scared me. I wasn't too sure of my sobriety—which is no doubt a good thing—and so spent the majority of my time fighting against the need to scratch that itch. While the itch has remained over all these years, my desire to scratch it has lessened. Now it's a matter of pride to wait it out, sort of like resisting the call of an old lover you know is bad for you. *You want me back, but I'm done with you.* Every time I resist, I get a little bit stronger. Besides, losing Bobby was what got me into sobriety to begin with; I'd be damned if I'd let finding him take it away from me. What sort of sense would that make?

I heard Martha in bits and pieces, her voice as calm and controlled as ever. Martha always was an old soul. There were times, when the boys were very young, I felt like asking Martha for advice. Even as a young girl she was together enough I felt lacking in her company. *Do you think he's hungry?* I wanted to ask when Bobby screamed. *What about that rash? Does it look any better to you?* Stupid, I know, and inappropriate, too. But I was a drug head, so what do you expect? It didn't take much back then for a person to have it *more together* than I did, even if that person was only six years old.

Now she made phone calls and poured tea and scribbled notes on a yellow notepad, and while I knew I should be paying attention, I couldn't. I vaguely remember the kids—Monique and Jason—no, Justin (how could I have forgotten that?)—coming home from school and greeting me with a quick peck on the cheek. I remember someone setting a plate in front of me, but whatever meal it held didn't register. I remember Ricky's voice, serious sounding, as the sun began to lower over the lake and a breeze picked up, the soothing alto of wind chimes next to my ear.

Mostly, though, what I remembered was Bobby. A bull in a China shop, my Bobby was. That child could break things I didn't even know could be broken. Too loud, careless, even thoughtless sometimes, driving me crazy more often than not. Bobby handing me a note from his kindergarten teacher, Bobby being led home by an angry neighbor, Bobby making Ricky cry. And all the while his plump cheeks pink and rosy, eyes sparkling, feet shuffling, hands fidgeting, too full of life for his little-boy body to contain it all. He'd driven me to distraction, my Bobby had, but oh, how I'd loved him. "He'll be the death of me," I used to tell Von and he nearly was, but not in the way I'd meant. And although his disappearance had nearly killed me, it'd saved me, too. I was at least smart enough to recognize that.

Chapter 11: Ricky

H ere."

I looked up to see Martha reaching toward me with a rocks glass of whiskey minus the rocks, and in spite of the events of the day, I had to smile. Martha and I had a history with whiskey. Or rather, *I* had a history with whiskey, and *she* had a history of watching me puke my guts out, the sorry end to my one attempt at teenage rebellion. I hadn't known that spring of my sixteenth year that Martha would be pulling into the Powers' driveway late on a Friday night for a weekend visit home from the University of Central Florida. For her part, she certainly hadn't expected to stumble across me, down on my knees behind the scrub oak taking what I thought were surely my last breaths. No one could possibly be as sick as I was and survive until morning.

"What the hell have you done?" Her sharp whisper had barely pierced through the pounding in my ears, and I might have panicked at being caught were it not for the fact I was too weak to move. "God, never mind. I can smell it from here. You're supposed to drink it, not bathe in it," she said, struggling to pull me up by my arm. "Well, *you're* not, but we'll talk about that later."

"Leave me alone," I managed to say, my clammy face pressed against her chest as she fought to maneuver me around the side of the house. Any other time I would have enjoyed that particular position, but that night the soft scent of perfume emanating from her cleavage was enough to trigger another round of dry heaves.

"You're disgusting," she'd said, gripping me under the arm with one hand while shoving my head to the side with the other, aiming my face away from her and pointing me toward the palmetto bushes along the backside property line.

When the last spasm subsided I slid to the ground and curled into a fetal position, too spent to worry about the fire ants and ground hornets that were as much a part of our lawn as the Bahia grass that refused to grow. Von and my mother may have been running the best plant nursery in central Florida, but their talents didn't extend to our home. True to stereotype, the horticulturalists had the worst yard on the street.

"I deal with plants all day," Von had once said by way of explanation. "That's the last thing I want to deal with when I get home. And anyway"—she'd pointed to the undeveloped land behind our little duplex—"that's natural beauty, right there. That's what Florida is all about." It was beautiful, in its own way. Sand pines, oaks, lyonia, saw palmettos, rosemary, scrub holly. But that wasn't a *lawn*. A lawn was supposed to look … mown.

We didn't even have houseplants. Once in elementary school when I'd wanted to grow sweet pea plants as a part of my science fair project, I'd been met with a resounding *no*—in stereo, no less, Aunt Von on one side, my mother on the other.

Standing over me as I moaned on the ground, Martha had sighed before I heard the crunch of her footsteps on dead grass fading into the distance. *Fine*, I remember thinking. *Leave me here alone to die.* I'd sunken into quite a drunken one-person pity party before I saw her feet in front of my face, two, then four, then merging into two again, and heard the squeak of one of our rusty patio chairs as she sat. I felt blessed coolness on my face, dripping through my hair and running over my scalp. "I'll stay with you for a while," she said, wiping my face with the most delicious cold washcloth, "but you're going to have some explaining to do in the morning. It was that Hawkins kid, wasn't it?" She didn't wait for an answer. "I told you not to be hanging around that kid. He comes from a rough family. When I was in school with his older brother …"

Her voice faded as I drifted in and out of consciousness. It *was* the Hawkins kid, as a matter of fact, and I agreed with her that his whole family was rough. Still, when a classmate dares you and tells you to stop being such a p—

"Shut it!" Martha yelled so loudly I nearly snapped back to sobriety. "You do *not* say that word, do you hear me?"

I hadn't realized I was speaking aloud, but I was having a hard time sorting the waving, spinning world into my known reality versus some sort of fourth dimension. "I'm sorry, Martha," I managed to say before bursting into tears, much to my embarrassment and Martha's annoyance.

Now Martha plopped down across from me on the couch, her own sweating glass dripping onto the thigh of her jeans, leaving dark blue circles on the faded denim. "I wasn't sure if you'd recovered sufficiently over the past fourteen years to give it another shot, but it's all I've got."

I wasn't sure, either, but the first sip went down warm and I started to relax for the first time all day. "Mom's asleep, then?" Martha and I had a longstanding unspoken agreement: Neither of us ever drank alcohol in front of our mothers. Truthfully, neither of us drank much alcohol, regardless, but at that moment I was thankful for the warmth spreading through my limbs.

"Doubtful," she replied, "but I don't think she'll be coming out to join us. She's got a lot to process. She's not in the mood for company. Hardly said a word all afternoon."

I had a lot to process, too, but Martha had always been my go-to person for that exercise. As if she's read my thoughts, she reached out and patted my leg. "How are you holding up? This has to be quite a shock for you, too."

"It's a shock for all of us," I said. "It's crazy, isn't it? I mean, after all this time, for him to turn up this way. I don't know what to think. Part of me feels terrible for him. I can't imagine what he must have gone through all these years to make him do something like that. My dad was a real piece of work. I always felt a little bad, you know, wondering why he left me behind, but this sort of cements the fact that I was the lucky one that day."

Martha turned to face me, leaning against the far arm of the couch. For a moment she didn't say anything, just held her glass in one hand, slowly spinning it around with the other. "So you assume he's innocent, then."

I was taken aback by her question. "Well, yeah. Don't you? I mean, you knew my dad better than I did. I barely even remember him. Can you imagine having had to grow up with that?"

"No." She shook her head. "He was pretty scary. Do you remember, after you guys moved into the duplex, how he'd come around banging on the door in the middle of the night, ordering your mom to let him in? My parents had to take out a restraining order. I was terrified of him. I just knew he was going to break in one night in a drug-fueled rage and kill us all."

"But that proves my point," I said. "I can't imagine what he must have done to Bobby over all these years to make Bobby"—I paused, uncomfortable with the words—"to make Bobby kill him, but from what little I remember, I think we can safely say Bobby is the victim in all this."

"I guess we'll find out tomorrow," Martha said. "The arraignment is bright and early, nine o'clock, the first case of the day. Is your mom going to be able to stay calm? Because if she isn't, she really shouldn't be there."

"No guarantees," I said, because I honestly didn't know. Hell, I didn't even know if *I* could remain calm. "But neither of us will be able to make her stay away."

"The media will be there," she said. "Oh, yeah," she continued, catching my look of surprise. "They've gotten wind. Mom said they're camped out along the street in front of the duplex. She's having a devil of a time keeping Dad calm. I can't blame them, though. It really is quite a story. A man kidnapped by his father as a young boy reappears twenty-five years later when he's arrested for murdering said father." She leaned forward to put her glass on the coffee table in front of us. "You might need to hire someone, Ricky. I don't think you or your mom are equipped to handle what's coming."

I hadn't known at the time how prescient those words would turn out to be, and I wonder, had I known, what I might have done differently. Maybe nothing; maybe everything. As it was, the words created enough discomfort for me to desire a change of subject. "So where's Ty?" I asked, setting my own glass down as well.

Martha stretched her legs out, propping her feet on the table, and leaned her head against the back of the couch with a sigh. "I have no idea," she said, resting the crook of her elbow on her forehead.

Martha's husband did some sort of sports multimedia work, something I never fully understood but which kept him on the road a great deal of the time. "You've given up trying to keep up with his itinerary?" I asked with a smile.

"No," she said. "But it aggravates his girlfriend when I try to track him down."

It took a moment for her words to sink in and another moment for me to formulate some sort of response. "Martha—"

She waved a hand dismissively in my direction before crossing her arms over her chest. "It's been a long time coming," she said. "I'm almost glad it's finally here."

I turned to look at her, *really* look at her, and was surprised by how tired she looked. The delicate skin under her closed eyes was shadowed, and for the first time I noticed the fine lines across her forehead, the deepened creases along her nose that seemed to pull her mouth into a frown.

"Martha," I said again, and while she didn't interrupt me the second time, I still found I had no idea what to say. Instead, I scooted over next to her and gathered her in an awkward hug, which, to my dismay, was greeted with an immediate flood of tears and a stifled sob. In all the years I'd known Martha I'd seen her in every emotional state imaginable, but I'd never seen her sob. I stroked her hair and let her cry it out against my chest, my emotions teetering somewhere between shock and concern. The Martha I knew didn't sob.

When the tears finally subsided she sat up and reached for a box of tissues on the end table. "Damn you, Ricky. I didn't want to cry." I moved back to my side of the couch to give her some space. *Don't crowd me, Ricky,* I could hear her voice from my childhood, chastising me when I hovered too close. Martha had always liked her space.

"What can I do, Martha? How can I help?"

"Just being here is enough," she said. "Listening to me and letting me cry. I work so hard to keep it together in front of the kids." She swiped almost angrily at a final tear escaping down her cheek. "They don't know everything, not the extent of it. Ty travels all the time, anyway, so having him gone really isn't any different for them. But we're going to have to tell them soon. Ty's already rented an apartment closer to the city. Closer to *her.*"

She downed the rest of her whiskey in one swift movement. "No wonder they got hooked," she said, swiping the back of her hand across her mouth. "This stuff'll either make you not care, or knock you out so you can't. Don't worry," she answered my unasked question. We'd always kept each other in check in regards to alcohol consumption. Or at least we had since my youthful binge. I think on some level we were both afraid of where it might lead. I don't know if addiction is learned, or if there's a genetic factor, but neither of us wanted to take any chances. "I bought it during an angry moment," she confessed. "One of those 'I'll show you' moments that hurts no one but yourself. Or myself, as the case may be."

"Does your mother know?" I asked. "I mean about the separation, not the whiskey."

She shook her head with a small smile, an acknowledgement of my clumsy attempt at relieving some of her sadness with my inadequate humor. "Not about either one. I haven't told her anything. She's got enough to worry about with my dad. I can't burden her with this, too. Anyway." She stood abruptly. "That's enough about this tonight. Make yourself at home, Ricky, as always. I'm going to bed. It's been a hell of a week, and tomorrow looks to be just as stressful, if in a different way."

I moved to stand and hug her goodnight, but she was gone before I reached my feet.

Chapter 12: Ricky

In spite of the late night, I was up shortly after sunrise. I hadn't slept well—I doubt any of us had—and the longer I tossed and turned, the more uncomfortable I became. I never had liked staying in someone else's house, not even as a kid. I always worried my presence was inconveniencing my host, whether the host was the exhausted, overworked father of a childhood friend, or the son of my oldest friend. I was uncomfortably aware that my presence meant Justin had spent what surely must have been an uncomfortable night on the floor of his sister's room. The Brooks family, while certainly not struggling, lived in a modest home with only one guest bedroom, which my mother had rightly taken.

Even worse was my discomfort in using someone else's bathroom for my own personal hygiene rituals. Once, when I was twelve or thirteen, I spent the night with a classmate, ostensibly to work on a school project but in reality, our goal was more nefarious. On a dare, Jake had managed to swipe a pack of cigarettes from the gym teacher's desk.

Smoking on school grounds had been banned for several years by that time, but Mr. Polk wasn't much of one for letting the "establishment" dictate the rules. It was a well-known fact he took regular smoke breaks in the stand of palms behind the cafeteria, and he'd even been known on occasion to take a drag or two while the rest of us were busy running our weekly mile around the busted, half-sunken track encircling the football field. Hell, the high school kids from across the street used to bum cigarettes off him in the parking lot.

Anyway, I don't know how Jake managed to talk his parents into letting a group of rowdy boys spend the night on a school night, fictitious school project or no, but he did. Jake was what was known as a latchkey kid back then, spending the hours between his own arrival home and that of his parents thinking up all sorts of creative ways to test the limits his Christian family imposed. The focal point of the built-in shelf gracing the home's interior entranceway may have been a copy of the Holy Bible, but the focal point behind the cover of the return air vent set in the wall *under* the shelf was a stash of Playboy magazines, at least for the time being. At various times Jake had hidden his stash behind the clothes dryer, in the access door to the bathroom's plumbing, and under his parents' mattress.

"What? They gonna check under their *own* mattress?" he'd asked when we expressed disbelief. "Hell, naw. It's *mine* they're always looking under." We had to admit it was brilliant, in its way.

A few months after our afternoon of smoking and gawking at boobs and mysterious nether regions, Jake's house would burn to the ground. Thankfully, no one was home at the time. "The fuse box," he said the next week at school, and we knew. "Guess it wasn't the best place." But that's an entirely different story.

We had two hours, Jake informed the group of us that afternoon—me, a bug-eyed boy we called Turtleneck, and Tommy, the Hawkins kid Martha was forever warning me about—before Jake's mom came home from her job at their church's daycare center. "Hey, Crackbaby," Jake called over to me as we trooped through the front door. I flushed pink at the nickname, but it was a small town and kids can be cruel. Besides, how could I, a kid just as guilty as any other of calling a bug-eyed boy Turtleneck, complain about being called Crackbaby? "Grab some matches out of the drawer in the kitchen, the one with the handle hanging off it." He jerked his head to the right as he knelt to open the air vent, and I took off in the general direction he seemed to have indicated.

It was weird, traipsing through Jake's empty house. As I walked by what I assumed must be his parents' bedroom I couldn't help but notice a pile of dirty laundry in the floor. A pair of men's white briefs, skid marks intact, graced the top of the pile. A flimsy pink nightgown was thrown across the bed. For some reason, the vulnerability of the scene made me uncomfortable and I hurried on.

Farther down the hall I passed what could only have been his sister's room. She was what, back then, we called a punker. Blue and pink hair, black eyeliner, studded dog-collar necklaces, black leather pants. She was older than we were, at least a junior in high school, and she was missing, had been for the better part of a year. A runaway, my mother said one summer morning at the nursery as she and Von switched off the morning news and gathered their shovels and clippers. I could tell my mother felt sorry for her, although I didn't understand why.

"There's a balance," Aunt Von had tried to explain when I asked. I was following behind, pulling the old rusty Radio Flyer wagon we used to transport fresh clippings to the various mulch piles. I hated that job—mulch piles smell to high heaven—but I was also the only kid my age earning a steady income, ten dollars per week. I was rich, and although I hated the work, I enjoyed the notoriety it brought me.

"On the one hand, you've got children whose parents don't care at all." She looked sideways at my mother as she said it, but my mother continued pruning a Japanese plum tree as if she hadn't heard. I knew only the bare bones of my mother's history and hoped Von would go on to explain, but she didn't. "And on the other, you've got parents who care so much they suffocate a child. You've got to have a balance," she said.

Jake's voice called me back to my task. "Hey, Crackbaby, quit jerking off in my sister's room and get a move on."

I wasn't jerking off, had no intention of jerking off, but I did have a strange fascination with the mystery surrounding his sister. I don't think it would take a mental health expert to figure out the reasons behind my fascination. Nevertheless, I averted my gaze from the various belts, boots, spiral-bound notebooks, and hairclips on her floor and hurried to the kitchen to retrieve the required matches.

Two hours, four Playboy magazines, approximately fifty-two boobs, and an entire pack of cigarettes later, Jake's mother came home to find me puking in their bathroom. I can still see the look of disgust that crossed her face before she closed the door and went in search of Jake.

All of this to say, I really hate using someone else's bathroom. *Tighten it up, Clark,* I can hear my old journalism professor say. *Too much extraneous crap. Get to the friggin' point, already. Tighten it up and you might be a halfway decent writer someday.* Easier said than done when one is trying to explain one's own life.

So extraneous crap aside, there I was, sitting on the side of Justin's bed, checking my phone and urgently trying to wish away my watery bowels—apparently I *hadn't* recovered sufficiently over the past fourteen years to give whiskey another shot —when I saw the news.

Bobby had escaped.

Chapter 13: Von

Martha called just as I managed to back through the crowd of reporters camping across the end of my driveway. It was a miracle I hadn't hit any of them, and a good thing they couldn't see what was in my heart as I steered clear of them. We'd had a terrible night, Ben and I, and the morning wasn't looking to be much better. I'd had to practically physically restrain him during the night he was so frightened by the people milling about in our street. "Who are they, Von?" he'd asked, over and over again. "What happened? Is it McDuffie?"

The question came from so far out in left field it took me a minute to follow. The race riots, he meant, down in Miami. Four police officers were acquitted of murder charges in the death of Arthur McDuffie, a black man who died of multiple skull fractures after a confrontation with police. But that was years ago, decades, back in 1980. We hadn't been there, hadn't had anything to do with the rioting, but we'd watched the news coverage like everybody else we knew, and had felt the same hopelessness they'd felt.

Oh, there may have been some talk about protesting in Sanford, marching to the courthouse in support of our brothers and sisters farther south, but that's all it was, was talk. Truthfully, I don't think any of us felt marching would make a hill of beans worth of difference, and I know for a fact some of our men were afraid they'd end up in the same shape as Arthur McDuffie. Still, there were a few news crews hanging out hoping for a story, small organizations, like the one Ricky works for, because all the big ones were in Miami. I suppose the cameras and microphones on the street must have taken Ben back to that time.

I tried to answer him honestly, but his past and present were so tangled together he couldn't keep it straight. "Bobby's right next door," he'd say one moment, only to follow it with, "Tampa, you say? After all these years? Well, don't that beat all."

I hadn't opened any of the window blinds that morning, hoping he might have forgotten the chaos of the night before. I was tempted to stay home for the day, leaving the nursery up to Ted, but I had things I needed to do and besides, we couldn't hide indefinitely and who knew how long the trial was going to last, or when it would even begin. I'd just buckled us both in and raised the garage door to a mob of reporters when my cell rang, offering a blessed distraction for Ben. "Grab it, honey, would you? I can't talk while I'm driving."

He tore his eyes away from the crowded sidewalk and I clicked "speaker" before shoving the phone into his hand. "It's Martha. Quick, now, before we miss it."

"Mom?"

"Nope, Dad," Ben yelled into the phone, grinning and holding it too close to his mouth. I winced in sympathy for Martha's ears. "You got Dad here. What's up, Baby Girl?"

I breathed a sigh of relief. I'd successfully maneuvered out of the drive and down the street, avoiding not only the reporters, but the mental meltdown Ben may well have had, had Martha not called at exactly the right time.

"Oh. Hi, Dad. Is Mom there?"

"Right here, baby. I'm driving, so Dad answered the phone. What's up?"

"Maybe I should call back …"

"It's okay, hon. Whatever it is, it's better than what we have here. Distraction can be a good thing. Your dad and I are happy to hear from you." I'd been hoping she'd catch my point, and she did.

"Is it bad?"

"Not good," I answered, knowing what she meant. "But hearing from you always helps. Now, what's up?"

"Hearing from me probably won't help today. Bobby seems to have escaped."

I have to admit, that was more than I'd bargained for. "Escaped? From jail?"

"Who's in jail?" Ben asked, gripping my arm, causing me to yank the steering wheel hard to the right. I struggled to regain control, barely missing a mailbox that looked as if it had seen more than its fair share of hits. "Martha's in jail? What the hell did she do? It's those queen palms, isn't it? I told her they were too close to the road. City gets the first twenty feet, is what I told her, but you know how stubborn Martha—"

"No, Dad, I'm fine," Martha interrupted him, her voice tinny over the miles. "And the palms are fine. Looking real good, actually. It's just some criminal, is all. Someone escaped from jail on the way to the courthouse. Work stuff, local gossip. No big deal."

Her words may have worked to calm her father, but they certainly didn't calm me. "Do they know what happened?" This was a tricky game, getting information without upsetting Ben.

"Overpowered a transport guard is what they're saying. Took his firearm. Details are pretty sketchy at this point."

"Oh, my God." I glanced at Ben, who sat frowning silently at the phone in his hand. I had no way of knowing how much he was processing. "What about cuffs? Leg irons? Aren't they chained up during transport?"

"They're cuffed," she said. "He was cuffed, but in front, not behind. Guards' discretion. They evidently didn't think he was too big of a threat. But this is just speculation, Mom. They aren't releasing much information."

"Not a threat? But he was arrested for murder!"

"The murder of a man with a history of violence and drug abuse," she reminded me. "A man who kidnapped him away from his mother and twin brother when he was just a little boy. It's a safe bet a lot of people—Tabby and Ricky included, by the way—see Bobby as the victim in all this. The media is having a field day. They love stories like this. Ricky's boss has been calling all morning."

"The guards," I said, almost afraid to ask. "Are they okay?"

"One is hospitalized in critical condition," she said.

"And the other?" I winced in anticipation.

"No," she said quietly. "He's not okay."

Dead? Sweet Jesus.

"Mom? Do you understand?" I understood she didn't want to upset her father with too many details. I didn't, however, understand any of what was happening.

Good God Almighty.

I took a deep breath, pulled the truck to the side of the road, crunching over abandoned takeout containers and soda bottles and working not to slide into the soggy ditch. "And Bobby?" I managed to ask.

"Why are we stopping here, Von? We can't stop in the middle of the road. Woman, you never could drive worth a damn." Ben reached over to put the truck in gear but I grabbed his hand, holding it tight between my own, willing the tears knocking at the back of my eyes to disappear.

"It's okay, Ben. I can't drive and talk on the phone. You know that isn't safe. We can take a minute to talk to Martha, can't we?"

"My baby girl." He smiled. "How you doing, Martha?"

"I'm good, Daddy," she answered, right on key as always. "How're you?" she asked her daddy, and I sent her a mental *thank you.*

"Good, Baby Girl. Real good. But your momma can't drive worth a damn."

Martha laughed. "Well, Daddy, she's just trying to keep you guys safe. I'll be over in a couple of weeks to see you, okay?"

"Always, Baby Girl. You come on over anytime, you hear? And bring those grandbabies with you."

"I will, Daddy, but they're hardly babies anymore. Justin is taller than you are, now."

"Well, I'll be. Is that right? You better bring him here before he grows up and leaves all of us behind."

"Two weeks, I promise. Hey, is Mom around?"

"I'm here."

"He's on the run," she answered my earlier question. "No sightings yet."

The world in front of me was spinning; I couldn't wrap my head around it.

"Mom." Martha's voice was insistent, cutting through the fog.

"What?" I made myself focus.

"If you were Bobby, where would you go?"

"Not here." My answer was immediate. "The media, cops, they're everywhere. This would be the last place he'd head for, Martha, so don't you worry about that. Besides, if he knows where we are, why didn't he come sooner? He's had all this time." I spoke the words I'd been thinking for the past twenty-four hours.

"I've thought that, too, and it only adds to my concerns," Martha said. "I don't know why he didn't come home, but I'm not so sure that isn't where he's headed now. That's where Tabby and Ricky are headed, too. They left a few minutes ago." I could hear the worry in her voice. "We don't know Bobby anymore, Mom. What we do know is that he's killed two men, with another barely hanging on. Whatever he's been through, whatever his dad did to him all those years doesn't matter right now. We can't let pity cloud our judgment."

Her words sent goose pimples down my arms.

"Be safe," she said. "And call me when we can talk more. Love you, Daddy," she added for Ben's sake.

"Love you, too, Baby Girl. You bring those grandbabies to see me. I mean it, now."

"I will, Daddy. Love you both." She disconnected.

"Well now," said Ben, all smiles. "That was nice, wasn't it? A call from my baby girl. Yes, sir, that's the way to start the day."

I begged to differ, given the reason for the call, but knew better than to say that. I turned the truck around to head back home. I hadn't been able to go to Tampa with Tabby, but I could at least meet her when she got home. Then Ben surprised me, as he so often does these days.

"I know you've hidden my guns from me," he said, leaning close over the console. "I imagine over at Tabby's somewhere. That's okay. Do what you need to do. I understand." He raised his brows when I glanced over at him. "Some days I'm not myself. I've got enough brains left to know that, although if I ever get so bad you think I'll hurt you, I hope you'll use one of those guns on *me*." He leaned back into his seat and patted my forearm, his hand rough from years of manual labor.

"Ben, I would never think—"

"It's okay, baby," he interrupted me. "You don't need to explain. But if you ever do use one on me, make it the Glock. I always have loved that pistol. It'd be a hell of a way to go."

"Ben! How can you even—"

"Easy, woman." He chuckled. "I was just trying to get a rise out of you."

"Well, it worked." I was annoyed, then. As much as I'd always loved bantering with Ben, I didn't find that conversation funny *at all*.

"But hear what I'm saying," he said, his voice turning serious, "because it's important, and you know as well as I do I might not remember it by the time we get home."

"I'm listening, Ben, but only if you knock this nonsense off."

"No nonsense here, Veronica. Listen to me. Get my guns back from Tabby. Hide 'em somewhere else. Tabby's place is not where they need to be right now." He held up a finger when I tried to speak. "Keep that shotgun loaded. Hide it from me if you need to, but keep it where you can get at it, and keep it loaded. I mean it, Von. I always told y'all that boy wasn't no angel."

Chapter 14: Tabby

I sat on the front stoop and thought about my life. Ricky had headed for his office after making sure I made it into the house okay without getting swarmed by reporters. His phone had rung constantly the whole time we'd been gone, his boss leaving ugly messages ordering him to pick up, but Ricky had refused. "Let him fire me," he'd said. "I'm not going to let him turn our lives into a circus." He'd dropped me off with a kiss on the cheek. "I'll be back tomorrow," he said. "Early if I no longer have a job, later if I do."

I'd spent the ride home from Tampa looking out the window, wondering where Bobby was. I searched the face of every pedestrian, peered into the car of every passing motorist. It was eerily reminiscent of when he'd first disappeared, when I'd take Ricky to the beach and leave him to his own devices while I spent every moment searching for Bobby among the other swim-suited children. Or when we'd go Christmas shopping at the mall and I'd take off running after someone who looked vaguely like Bobby—like

Ricky, the child I drug along behind me as I ran after the ghost of his brother. I rode home alongside Ricky, my mind elsewhere as I continued to look for Bobby.

Von had met me in the driveway, hugging me, holding me away to look at me, then pulling me close to hug me again. She'd finally had to leave to tend to Ben, who'd peered out the door at me as if he didn't even know who I was. I could hear her through the open door, the one that leads out onto our shared porch. "Ben," she was saying, "come sit down, honey. Let's see what's on T.V." Ben was cranky; I could hear him muttering and fussing, although I couldn't tell what he was saying.

It was terrible, what was happening to Ben, but maybe even more terrible what was happening to Von. I could hear how tired she was, and how sad, too. She wouldn't have ever admitted it, but she didn't have to. It was right there, in the way her mouth pulled down and her forehead creased.

There was no privacy at our little duplex, never had been, but that had been okay. Secrets meant failure for an addict, or so I'd once heard. There was no chance of keeping secrets in our shared space, and that was for the best. Von, Ben, Martha, they were family. More family—better family—than I'd ever had anywhere else. I loved them with my whole heart. Even so, I was glad to have the stoop to myself. I needed to get my thoughts in order.

The cicadas were loud that morning. *Diceroprocta olympusa*, I remembered, a strange thing to remember, especially for someone whose education was as spotty as mine, but I'd once been scared witless by one. It was at one of the foster homes; I could no longer remember their names, but I did remember they had no air conditioning. It was early August, before school started, and it was sweltering. There were two other foster children in the tiny house, sisters, younger than I was. The three of us shared a bedroom crammed with a set of bunks and an extra twin bed shoved so close to the closet door that I, being the skinniest in spite of my age, was the only one who could squeeze through the crack to fetch whatever clothes we needed.

I suppose it should seem sad I don't remember names, but that's what happens when you move around a lot as a kid. There were too damned many names to remember; there was no point even trying. Six months here, a year there, two weeks somewhere else until one foster mother decided it was too much work, after all. To this day, I don't know what the hell she was expecting. I was damaged goods; didn't they make that clear in the file? Anyway, whatever the reason, I always knew a move was coming and it was easier to keep my distance.

Only once had I made a point of remembering, and that was just after my sixteenth birthday. I remember how old I was because we'd had a cake, and after that, my foster mother had taken me and my social worker to the DMV for my driving test. I'd never in a million years expected anything like that. I was in heaven.

Of course it didn't last. The night I learned I had to move again, I'd written my foster parents' names down on the inside cover of my cardboard suitcase with a leaky ballpoint pen. At least that time I wasn't moving because I'd done something wrong or because they'd decided fostering troubled kids was more than they could handle, though that was small comfort to me. That time, it was because my foster mother's father was dying, and she was moving across the country to be with him in his final days.

I was devastated to lose them; they'd been kind to me, the closest I'd ever come to having a normal childhood complete with normal parents. For the brief time I lived there, I'd developed a sense of hope I'd never before felt, a glimpse into what my life could have been like under different circumstances. Even a belief that maybe one day, it could still be that way for me.

I cried the entire night before the move; my eyes were nearly swollen shut when the social worker came to pick me up the next morning. "We'll stay in touch," my foster mother had said, embracing me. "We love you, Tabby. You're like a daughter to us." I returned the hug, inhaling the lemony scent of her hair, before climbing into the social worker's rattle-trap car to be driven to the next in a string of new homes.

Naturally, they didn't keep in touch. I never heard from them again. Once, after I was grown and shuttled out of the system, I sent a letter to their old address on the off chance they may have returned to Florida. I never heard back, and I never attempted contact again. The plain truth of the matter is that sometimes other people mean more to us than we do to them. They touch us in some way, but that doesn't mean we touch them back. Sometimes, it's better to just accept that and move on.

Now, all these years later, I no longer remember their names, either.

Anyway, I was probably around ten that summer, the summer of the cicada and the air-condition-less foster family whose names I also no longer remember. I was old enough to have almost forgotten my mother's face, another tidbit that should probably be sad, but given the facial expression that stuck in the front of my mind—the one she wore when she poured vinegar down my throat or made me kneel on gravel for hours—I was glad she showed up less and less in my nightmares. A few years later I'd discover cocaine, which made her memory—hell, *all* memories—just about disappear, but that summer I was still battling the demons honestly.

If I occasionally missed my mother, I was smart enough by that time to realize it wasn't really her I missed but the idea of who I'd wanted her to be. You know, the young, smiling mom with red lipstick who wears an apron and greets her kids with a plate of homemade cookies and a glass of cold milk when they get home from school. But that had never been my mother—for all I knew, that was nobody's mother—and since she was dead, the fantasy stood no chance of becoming reality.

And she was most certainly dead; of that I had no doubt, since I was the one who found her. Dead of an overdose, I later learned, and I can tell you this: that tragic, beautiful woman you see in the movies? The one who finally seems to be at peace, who simply slipped away to a better place? That is *not* what it's like. No, ma'am. My mother's dead face was as angry as ever in that nasty-assed tub, loose shit floating in the cold water and throwing shadows over her white belly while vomit dried in her hair.

I didn't have a father, or at least not one I knew, although there was a man I sometimes pretended was my father. He brought me sweets on the nights he visited my mother, telling me to be a good girl while he and my mother visited. I'd sit curled in the corner of my room sucking on butterscotch candies while listening to the sound of her headboard banging against the wall. Another sad point, I suppose, wishing the only one of my mother's friends who treated me decently could be my father. I saw him only once after she died, and that was at her funeral. I tried to get his attention, even tried to run after him, but by then I was already in the system, an orphaned girl with no one to take care of her. The social worker shut me up with an angry shake, and the man who hadn't abused me left without seeing me.

By the time I'd been moved to the cramped little house with the quiet old couple and two broken girls, I'd come to believe I was cursed, which is why at lights-out, when I heard the vibrating, buzzing sound under my bed, I didn't move. The window had been open all day, and although there was a screen in place, it was so tattered and torn it wasn't much help at keeping out anything that wanted to come in. Palmetto bugs were around every corner, crawling in from the stack of old wood behind the house. We were all terrified of them, doing rock-paper-scissors to figure out which of us had to smack one with a shoe, their nasty musk making us gag when we cleaned up the pulpy splatter they left behind. Lizards, too, were everywhere. The foster mother would yell at us to catch them and set them outside, then yell at us again to pick up their wiggling tails when they dropped them on the way out.

Given all that, it wasn't a stretch to think there was a rattler under my bed, and not a pygmy, either. It was big, a diamondback; I was sure of it. The buzzing sound was loud, seeming to get louder by the second. I didn't move. I'd spent the majority of my life attempting to avoid trouble by becoming invisible. It was an ingrained defense mechanism by that time; I never even thought about running. Whatever was going to happen would happen; I could make it easy or hard. I chose easy. The buzzing only intensified as I waited for it to strike, until the sound finally caught the attention of one of the other girls, the smaller one who slept on the bottom bunk across from me.

All hell broke loose after that, their reaction freeing me from my self-induced paralysis, the three of us screaming and crashing into each other in the dark until our foster father threw open the door with a .22 Ruger in hand. We were naïve in those days. We didn't typically worry about boogeymen creeping in through open windows, but Dean Corll, the Candy Man, was all over the news that week for killing twenty-eight boys in Texas. God only knows what our poor foster father expected when he heard three terrified girls shrieking in the middle of the night.

What he got, once he shooed us out of the room, was a cicada which, apparently tired of the ruckus, flew out from under my bed and landed in his beard, the end result of which was a wildly fired off shot into the ceiling, a string of curse words, and a double shot of bourbon.

While he calmed his nerves in the living room, the foster mother got us all a drink of water and tucked us back into bed. They were decent people; I wish I could remember their names, but I can't. It's interesting how I remember everything my mother ever did to me, every specific way she hurt me, but I can't even remember the names of the people who were kind.

I've heard about people who forget their bad memories, but I unfortunately wasn't one of them. Ask me how many times my mother ripped the hair from my head for what she called "bein' prissy," and I can tell you exact numbers. *You feelin' pretty, little girl? I'll slap the pretty right off your fuckin' face.*

I remember every time she burned my feet with a cigarette lighter for running in the house—as if running could have somehow damaged the shitholes we lived in—every time she swabbed my mouth out with bleach for sassing, and every time she slapped my ears for not listening—hard to forget that one, since I'm mostly deaf in my right ear. But for the life of me, I cannot remember the name of the woman who tucked us back into bed that night and told us about cicadas.

"*Diceroprocta olympusa*," she said. "Cicadas are magical. Do you believe that?"

I don't recall what my foster sisters said, if anything. As for me, I didn't respond at all. I didn't want to disrespect the foster mother by disagreeing. I knew full well by then there was no such thing as magic, but I wanted her to stay. I wanted to hear her story. I didn't even care what it was about. I was ten years old, and it was my first bedtime story ever.

"They used to be people," she said. "Cicadas did, or so the story goes." She reached over to push the hair out of my eyes and I stiffened at her touch. She either didn't notice, or pretended not to. "A long time ago, way back before radios and records existed," she said, "the goddesses introduced people to music. The people loved it so much they danced and sang all day and all night. They danced and sang so long, in fact, they forgot to eat and starved to death."

It wasn't exactly the happily-ever-after story I'd been hoping for, but it caught my interest, relatable as it was. Starvation was something I understood.

"It's said that the goddesses rewarded them by turning them into cicadas. Now they can sing all day and night without having to eat, or so the story goes," she said.

"Is that a true story?" one of the sisters asked, and the foster mother laughed.

"Well," she said, "that depends on whether or not you believe in magic. Some people think cicadas bring good luck," she continued, tucking in a sheet. "They stand for new beginnings. That's because after they're born they crawl into the ground where they live for a long time. When they're ready, they crawl back up and shed their old skin, flying away with new wings. When you see a cicada, it means you're about to start a new life."

"So Tabby is about to start a new life," the sister said, "since it was under her bed."

The foster mother turned to look at me. I couldn't read her expression in the shadows. "I hope so," she said. "I hope that's exactly what that means." She turned off the light. "Get some sleep," she said. "We've got school shopping tomorrow. It's going to be a long day."

Forty-some-odd years later as I sat on the porch listening to cicadas, I wondered what sort of new life might be in store for me. Bobby was alive. I'd waited for him all those years, refusing to move, to change even so much as the paint on their bedroom walls, much to Ricky's annoyance. But it was finally going to pay off, because Bobby was going to come home. I could feel it in my bones. I didn't know what had kept him away from me all that time, but I wouldn't have put anything past Vernon. Who knew what lies he might have told? For all we knew, Bobby may have thought we were dead. I'd said as much to Ricky on the drive home.

"But he knows, now," I'd told him. "With the media everywhere, the stories being played over and over again, now he knows we're here, right where we always were. He'll come home."

Ricky hadn't anything for a full minute, signaling to pass a semi in front of us before settling back into the middle lane. Then he'd shot me a quick look. "What if he does?" he'd asked. "What if he does come home? What will you do?"

"What do you mean, what will I do? I've waited all this time for him to come home, Ricky. So have you."

He'd stared straight ahead, chewing on his lips the way he'd always done when he had to say something he knew I wouldn't like. "He's wanted by police, Mom. If Bobby shows up, you have to call the police. You know that."

I'd turned in my seat to look at him. "You want me to call the police who ignored us all these years," I'd said, my voice rising. "The police who didn't have time to fool with an addict, the ones who couldn't seem to find him even though he was only *two fucking hours* away this whole time. *Those* police? *Those* are the ones you want me to call? So they can do what, take him away again? Tell me, Ricky, is that what I'm supposed to do? I'm curious to know."

He hadn't answered, and I was immediately sorry for raising my voice to him, for using those words. I'd tried to apologize but he'd waved it away. "It's all good, Mom. We'll figure it out. Just be careful, okay? Promise to call me if you hear anything, if you get any indication at all that he's in the area. Okay? Promise?"

"I'm sorry, Ricky." I'd picked up his hand from the gearshift where it rested between us and given it a squeeze. "I'm so sorry, honey. I'm just ... I don't even know what to think." He'd squeezed back, and I'd wondered if he'd noticed I hadn't promised. I didn't want to lie to Ricky. I hadn't lied to anybody since getting sober, and I didn't want to start now. The truth was, I didn't know what I would do if Bobby showed up. I couldn't think past the possibility of my boy coming home.

The door creaked behind me and Von held a cup of coffee out to me, which I gratefully accepted. "Where's Ben?" I asked.

She groaned, her knees popping as she lowered herself to the stoop beside me. "Watching the television," she said. "Yelling at *Matlock* on the Hallmark Channel. Thank God for cable. You know he always did love Andy Griffith; still calms him right down. Thought I'd take a minute to catch my breath while he and Ben Matlock solve some crimes. How're you doing, honey?"

"Did I ever tell you the story of the cicadas?" I asked, holding the coffee under my nose and inhaling the strong scent.

"Maybe once or twice," Von said, nudging me with her shoulder. "But go ahead and tell me again."

That's what happens when you've known someone for years; you end up repeating stories, even though you know you've already told them. I suppose sometimes when we're stuck in our memories we want someone to be there with us. If we're lucky, we have that someone. I was lucky.

Chapter 15: Ricky

I knew my mom, and I highly suspected if Bobby did happen to show up, she'd keep him hidden. It wasn't that my mother was a lawbreaker; it was more that she'd led a life that taught her not to trust the system. And she had a good point, I had to concede that. The police had never managed to find Bobby, had never had a single clue, or at least not one they'd shared with us. Had she been someone else, someone more financially stable, more socially influential, would they have expended more effort in their search? It's impossible to know, and while I respect our local law enforcement as much as the next guy, I couldn't blame her for doubting the system, especially considering her crappy childhood.

Then there was this: While I knew my mother loved me, Bobby was the missing piece, and isn't that always the most important one? After all, no one looks for the piece that's already there. I couldn't imagine any way she'd give him up, not after all those years of waiting. With one hand on the wheel, I wrestled my cell from the pocket of my jeans, scrolled to Martha's number, and dialed.

"I hope you're not driving," she said, but she knew I was. It was a terrible habit of mine, born from speeding to developing news stories and rushing to make deadlines.

"It's not against the law yet," I said by way of excuse, "at least not in Florida."

"Good luck with that defense when you kill someone," she said. "Pull over if you want to talk. Otherwise, I'm hanging up."

I checked the rearview mirror before pulling off to the side of Highway 415. No-nonsense Martha. I loved that about her. "So what do you think?" I asked.

"I think McElwain is the right guy," she said. "The Gators are past due—"

"Very funny," I interrupted. "About Bobby. Do you think he's headed this way?"

"I think it's within the realm of possibility," she said carefully. "Have you pulled over?"

"Relax," I assured her. "I'm on the side of the road watching a couple of buzzards clean up roadkill, which seems eerily symbolic of what's going to happen when I make it into the office this morning."

"Charming," she said. "You seriously need to get out of that place. You can do better, Ricky. But what about you? Do you think he'll try to reach your mother?"

"I would think that," I said, "except for the reporters. Police, too. They're all over Mom's street, or at least they were when I dropped her off. I can't see how he could make contact with all that going on."

"He's used to hiding," she said. "Think about it for a minute. He's been in hiding for over twenty-five years, at least twelve of those as an adult."

I wasn't sure what to make of that. A part of me still clung to the belief that our father had somehow tricked him, brainwashing him into thinking we were dead, or gone, or … something. Another part wondered if he'd been so abused and mistreated he could no longer think properly. Hey, it happens. Crazy thoughts, maybe, but otherwise, there really was no explanation for his continued absence other than to accept he hadn't wanted to come home.

Right?

"What do you think she'll do?" Martha asked. "If he contacts her, I mean."

"She'll protect him," I said without hesitation.

"But Ricky, he's a murderer. He's a criminal. He's not the Bobby we knew."

"He's still her baby," I countered. "The missing piece of her heart. No way she'll turn him in."

"Then you'd better keep an eye on her," she said. "She could be in real danger, whether from him, or from the people searching for him. Ricky, at best she'd be harboring a fugitive."

"And at worst?"

I could hear her breathing before she answered. "Well," she said, "he killed your father, didn't he?"

"Yeah, but he—"

"He *what*, Ricky? You don't know. For all you know, he was the epitome of a perfect father. For all you know, he attended Little League games, taught Bobby how to knot a tie, and bought him his first car. *You don't know.*"

"He was an asshole," I said. "You know that. He was an abusive, drug-addicted asshole."

"Your mother was an addict, too," she said softly. "So was mine. People can change. People *do* change. Maybe Vernon changed. My point is, we don't know. Maybe the man Bobby killed was a completely different man from the one we knew. All we know at this point is that Vernon is dead, and Bobby is the one who killed him."

"You can't seriously think," I began, but stopped.

"You can't seriously not," she said. "Now, I have to go. Ty keeps buzzing in."

"That's good, right?" I asked, painfully aware of how self-centered our conversation had been. Martha was having a rough go of it, too.

"Depends on your perspective," she said. "He served me with divorce papers right after you left. I'll talk to you later, Ricky. Keep me posted."

"You, too," I said, but she'd already disconnected.

Chapter 16: Ricky

I wasn't fired, at least not yet, but only because Andy wanted me to be the feature story in a special edition he also wanted me to work overtime to get to press. I was sure there was a joke in there somewhere—a joke other than me, I mean—but I was too worn out to follow that train of thought. Instead, I poured myself a cup of coffee-sludge and headed to my cubicle, all without giving Andy an answer. An answer didn't seem necessary, anyway, since technically he hadn't asked a question. My coworker, Gerry, accosted me halfway to my desk and I very nearly turned around to head back to Andy. That's what my day was shaping up like.

"Dude," Gerry said, stopping in front of me in the corridor, palms up. His questions were obvious, but for whatever petty reason, I didn't want to acknowledge them. I was tired, irritable, and confused, so I waited, eyebrows raised as if I had no idea what he wanted from me. "So?" he finally asked, lightly punching my chest for emphasis. "What's the deal?"

Gerry wasn't a bad guy. He was actually a pretty decent reporter. I'd once asked him why he stayed with Andy's shitty little organization and he'd said, "ROI, baby. Return on investment. Decent paycheck, little work. It's all about quality of life." He could have been right; maybe he *was* right, but I'd never been able to master enjoying my quality of life while knowing I spent my days writing crap barely disguised as news. The airwaves were polluted enough without my adding to the problem.

Anyway, my point is my reaction to Gerry that morning had nothing to do with Gerry. He was the same boisterous, slightly obnoxious, overly friendly guy he'd always been. We'd always been if not friends, exactly, certainly friendly. But he was annoying the hell out of me, and something about his brotherly thump on the chest sent me over the edge. I grabbed his wrist, twisting it slightly as his mouth dropped open in obvious surprise.

"None of your fucking business," I replied, then using his twisted arm as a lever, shoved him to the side and continued to my cubicle. I heard him stumble against the wall, thrown off balance by the push, but I didn't look back to see. Later, I'd feel terrible about the way I'd treated him. I'd never been a violent person, never been a bully, never wanted to draw attention to myself. But later, it would be too late. Whereas at one time Gerry would have handled our story with kid gloves, my little tantrum in the corridor ensured he'd go after us full force. I couldn't blame him.

At some point in the coming days I may have even felt exonerated, as if being drug through the mud myself might make up for all the times I'd done it to others through my lousy excuse of a job. Of course, I'd failed to take into account the effect it would have on my loved ones. As for Gerry, his reporting on my life's drama would ultimately get him out of that place. By the end of it all, when every ounce of gossip and speculation had been reported *ad infinitum*, he was offered a much more lucrative position with one of the supermarket tabloids. *ROI*, I could hear him saying. *Decent paycheck, little work*. But that was later.

That day as I angrily whipped my seat away from my desk I heard him cursing me. "God*damn*, Clark, what the hell is wrong with you? You nearly broke my arm!"

It was a fair question. What the hell was wrong with me? Well, my life had just been turned upside down and ass-backwards, and it pissed me off to be greeted as if I were—are you ready for this?—tabloid fodder. Poetic justice at its best, right? At that moment, I was tempted to quit my job, pack up my desk, and walk away, but something stopped me, and that something was Andy.

His offer, although both of us knew it wasn't really an offer: he would allow me to keep my job if I could persuade my mother to give *Swamplands* an exclusive interview, complete with a sidebar from me. It was tempting, not because I needed the job, although I did, but because what Andy was really offering me was some measure of control. My mother's story would come out regardless, was already coming out, but as I well knew, the only chance we had to manage the telling of it would be to grant an interview. Andy was giving us that chance not out of the goodness of his heart, but because he wanted the scoop. Still, if we could benefit from it, it was an opportunity worth taking, or so I believed at the time.

In hindsight, I realized I'd underestimated not only Andy's lack of morals, but also the extent of Gerry's anger toward me. Given my choices at that moment, I'd felt the best course of action was to call my mother and persuade her to do the interview as soon as possible, preferably that afternoon. I wasn't looking forward to the call, but did believe it would provide her some small measure of protection against the onslaught of ugly internet trolls and armchair psychologists who were bound to climb onboard the avalanche of our lives. It was in that state of mind that I picked up the phone and set in motion a chain of events for which I would never forgive myself, and from which I would never fully recover.

Chapter 17: Tabby

When Ricky first called me about coming to his office for an interview, I thought he'd lost his mind. I was proud of Ricky, don't get me wrong. I know he didn't grow up in the easiest of circumstances, but he'd always kept his grades good, earning himself a scholarship to Stetson where he'd majored in journalism. I also knew he wasn't proud of the job he'd had since graduating, but I thought he was being too hard on himself. "All of us have to start somewhere," I used to tell him. "You have to work your way up."

And I'll tell the truth about this, too: I'm as guilty of gobbling up tabloid gossip as the next person. Von and I both took the *Swamplands*, partly so we could read whatever Ricky wrote, but also so we could sit over our morning coffee out at the nursery and cluck and shake our heads at the crazy things people do. Maybe that wasn't nice of us; I'm sure it wasn't, but we hadn't meant any harm. Sometimes, especially if things might not be going exactly the way we hoped they might, it offered a small measure of comfort to take a look around and think, *Well, at least I don't have that going on.* It wasn't about taking pleasure in someone else's pain—Von and I would never do that—it was more about reassuring ourselves that things in our little corner of the world weren't so bad, after all.

I knew exactly how other people would react to my story, a woman who had her child stolen right out from under her while she was drunk. And I *was* drunk, it's true. There's this thing we addicts do, especially when we're heavy in the disease. We put things on a scale, like, *But I'm not shooting up*, or, *I don't do street drugs.* Anything to put ourselves a little step above the *real* addicts, or so we think, because we don't want to believe that's us. That's where I was back then.

I was off the blow, had been since that morning in the emergency room when the doctor looked at me as if he'd need to go bleach his eyeballs when he was done with me. I'd been off the sauce, too, for a long time, but the thirst had slowly crept back up on me until one day I gave in and bought a six pack. God, it was good going down, cold and satisfying, especially after a crazy-hot day out at the nursery. I drank three after the boys were in bed, then wrapped the empty bottles in newspaper and hid them deep in the bottom of the trash. That night I slept like a baby, and the next day I bought another six pack. And so it went, until beer didn't have the desired effect and I went for something stronger. By that time, I couldn't hide it from Von and Ben and nearly took their heads off if they even mentioned my drinking. I didn't want to hear it. It's hard to be in denial when someone is always in your face telling you you're a drunk.

I don't know how long I would have gone on that way or where it might have ended if Bobby hadn't been taken. Here's another bit of truth for you, just in case you were starting to feel sorry for me: I don't know if I'd have gotten sober even then, had Von not done what she did. I might very well have used Bobby's disappearance as an excuse to fall even deeper into my addiction.

When Von brought the sheriff's deputies to my side of the duplex about a week after Bobby disappeared and found me drunk off my ass, snot smeared all over my face from crying, she sobered me up by smacking me hard across the face. "Look at Ricky," she said, so I did. He was sitting on the floor holding a half-full bottle of beer. Had he had a drink? I don't know. To this day, I don't know. "These men are here to talk to you about Bobby," said Von, pushing her face right up against mine. "They need to ask you some questions about Vernon. Sit up and answer them. I'll take Ricky. And Tabby"—she grabbed my cheeks to make sure I was looking at her—"I'm not bringing him back." Her forehead was scrunched up and her eyes were hard the way they always get when she's mad. "When you get done with the deputies, pack your stuff and get out of my house." Through it all, the deputies never said a word, just watched and waited.

Well, that did it. I got sober. I'd lost one child; I couldn't lose another plus the rest of my family on top of it. Von had done it from a place of love, I knew that, and not just love for me, but for Ricky, which was even more important. It was what I had needed her to do. It wasn't easy, but when she saw I was serious, Von stuck by me like she always had, and so did Bob Linwood and the rest of the gang from over at the church.

If Ricky's paper got hold of that ugly history, it'd be all over the internet by morning. I knew that without a doubt. And people would do exactly what Von and I had always done; they'd cluck and shake their heads and thank their lucky stars they'd never been foolish enough, careless enough, or even bad enough to bring that kind of luck down on themselves. I could see the comments already. *It would serve her right if he found her after all these years and shot her, too*, or maybe, *Kid didn't stand a chance, with those two losers as parents.*

"It'll be all over the internet, anyway," Ricky had said, "and quicker than you think. There are no secrets these days, Mom. It'll come out, and we're already on borrowed time. At least this way you can tell the story your way."

"My way doesn't make it any better, Ricky."

"Look, Mom, you had a terrible childhood and when you were thrown out into the adult world with no safety net, you made some mistakes. Okay? How could you not have? You'd never had a role model; no one ever taught you how to be an adult. But you worked hard to make it right, and you did. You're a good mother. A great mother. People need to see that. If the story is going to go viral, at least make it the one you told."

The *viral* part of what he'd said struck me more than anything. If the story went viral, would Bobby see it? If he knew for sure I was still here, missing him, loving him, waiting for him, would he come home?

That was what finally made me agree to do it, and it wasn't bad, nothing like what I'd expected. I made it to the offices of *Swamplands* in less than half an hour, traffic on I-4 being more manageable during early afternoon hours. The receptionist took me right to Andy, Ricky's boss, who greeted me with an unexpected hug. Ricky stayed with me the whole time, and Andy couldn't have been any nicer. He led us into a nice room with a couch and some wingback chairs, and he had someone bring me coffee and a bagel.

"I know you must be missing lunch to do this," he said, "so let me at least feed you. I appreciate you coming in on such short notice. We want the story out first thing in the morning, before sunrise."

He was gentle with his questions and sympathetic when I answered them. He didn't judge me at all; I imagine he'd heard enough stories from desperate people by then to be used to just about anything.

"That wasn't bad," I told Ricky when we'd finished, while he walked me to my car. "He's a nice man, isn't he?"

Ricky stopped walking and put his hands on my shoulders, turning me to face him. "No, Mom. He's not a nice man. He does what he has to do to get the story. I appreciate the way he treated you, but don't forget for a minute that it's the story he wants."

"Well, anyway," I said, a little surprised by Ricky's reaction, "it could have been a lot worse. Are you coming by this evening?"

Ricky shook his head. "Andy's got a few questions for me, too. He wants to hear the brother's perspective, I suppose, but there isn't much I can tell him. Plus, Gerry took off early, so I'll be working overtime to get the special edition out on time." He leaned down and kissed me on the cheek before opening the car door for me. "At least I still have a job. I'll call you tomorrow morning. Put me on speaker when I do, so I can listen to you and Aunt Von while you read the paper."

He knew us so well. "Call me early," I said. "You know Von and I will be up at sunrise looking for it."

"Yes, ma'am, I know that," he said with a smile. "Be careful driving home."

I returned his smile. "How many times have I said that to you over the years? Am I officially old now? We're doing a role reversal."

"Don't forget to eat your vegetables," he said, gently closing the car door and waving before turning to walk back to his office.

God, how I loved my boys. I wanted to see them together again, *Double Trouble*, as Ben had always called them. "How's Double Trouble doing today?" he'd ask in the evenings when he got home from the nursery. After Bobby disappeared, Ben's greeting had morphed into "How's it going, Ricky-boy?" the double having turned singular.

I truly believed if Bobby would just come home, we'd get everything sorted out. We'd be able to fix it; we'd be able to make people understand. I had no doubt he'd killed his father in self-defense. I didn't know what had happened with the cops, why he'd turned on them the way he had, but I didn't have a lot of trust for anyone who worked in the system. My experience had always been they weren't around when you needed them, but were damned near everywhere when you did something wrong. No, I didn't trust them. I wanted to hear from Bobby. I needed to know his story. More than anything else, I just wanted him to come home.

Chapter 18: Von

I couldn't find Ben. I'd looked out my office window to see dark clouds rolling in from the coast, and decided to take Ben home while Ted closed up shop. The incoming storm meant no customers for the rest of the day and besides, I knew Tabby would be home soon and I wanted to hear all about her interview.

Those decisions made, I'd stepped down from the trailer and headed toward the sego palms, which Ben had spent the afternoon fertilizing. He'd had a good nap when Tabby left, and awakened sharp, energetic, and ready to get to work. The twists and turns of Ben's illness could be exhausting, but I'd learned to treasure the moments I was allowed to have my husband back.

I didn't immediately worry when I rounded the trailer to find a wheelbarrow full of mulch and a shovel, but no Ben. I had no reason to worry, or hadn't up to that point. He knew the nursery every bit as well as I did, and while he might have become confused a time or two, mentally traveling back in time to the days when we lived there, he'd certainly never wandered off or given me reason to fear for his safety.

I didn't really start to worry until I'd circled the entire perimeter with no sight of him. The wind was picking up by then, and thunder rumbled in the distance. Thunderstorms are fast and furious in central Florida, and the lightning they bring kills an average of nine people each year, more than anywhere else in the country, or so the weatherman says, and I wasn't about to argue with him. I needed to find Ben and get both of us inside.

But Ben was nowhere to be found. I circled the perimeter again, then crisscrossed through it, yelling for Ted to leave the tractor where it was and come help me. Together we covered every single inch of the property, sheets of rain drenching us, wind nearly blowing us off our feet. We searched the sheds, the trailer, the vehicles, and the ditch. We crossed the highway and fought our way through the brambles and briars of undeveloped county land. All the while, lightning flashed so close our skin tingled; I could see the goosebumps on Ted's arms and felt the hair stand up on my own.

"Von," Ted was yelling at me over the deafening crash of thunder, and I knew he was telling me we had to get inside, it was too dangerous to continue looking, but I couldn't leave Ben behind. I pulled away from him, shielding my eyes from the rain to peer into the distance, frantically searching for a glimpse of Ben's white t-shirt.

I'd been so thankful that morning when he hadn't argued with me, hadn't slipped on a winter shirt when

I wasn't looking. He'd been so distracted by the reporters lined up along our street he'd barely spared me a glance when I laid out his clothes and coaxed him, one stiff leg at a time, into his jeans. *I'm in my own little world*, the t-shirt said, *but it's okay; they know me here.* The irony of the slogan hadn't escaped me that morning, but the shirt was an old one, a gift from Martha years before any sign of Ben's illness had been evident. It had always been one of his favorites. "From my little girl," he'd tell people who remarked on it. "My baby girl got me this."

Ted gripped my shoulders from behind, his mouth close to my ear, shouting over the storm. "We need to call the sheriff," he said, and my heart thudded in tandem with the thunder. "We're wasting time looking. We need to call the sheriff and get some help."

He was right. While we floundered around in a panic, Ben could be anywhere, hurt, scared, confused. I nodded, and he took off for the office at a sprint, with me limping along behind as quickly as my knees would allow.

Chapter 19: Tabby

I arrived home to find the street nearly empty of reporters; only a couple of stragglers remained, hidden in their vans away from the downpour. I didn't know if the storm had chased the others off, or if word had gotten out about my interview with Andy, but either way, I was glad to see them gone. Von's truck was gone, too, which surprised me a little. I'd expected her to be home. Nurseries see their busiest days on sunny afternoons; folks don't tend to be out looking for plants in the middle of a thunderstorm.

Maybe she and Ben had hunkered down in the trailer back at the nursery, I decided. Von had taken over all the driving months before, not making a big deal of it, just climbing into the driver's seat before Ben got a chance. She wasn't too wild about driving in the rain, and besides, there was always something to do out there: ordering, cleaning, repairing equipment. I'd done such a good job of convincing myself she and Ben weren't home that I nearly jumped out of my skin when I ran up the steps to see her standing there waiting for me.

"He's gone," she said, and something in her voice pulled me up short.

"Who's gone?" I asked, skidding on the wet porch. For a second I thought she meant Bobby, and my heart nearly stopped. Gone? Was she trying to tell me he'd been——?

"Ben," she said. "I can't find him." I nearly collapsed from relief, but then Von's voice broke on a sob, and I threw my umbrella aside to fold her in a hug. She leaned against me, sniffling into my shoulder. First Bobby, now Ben. What in heaven's name was going on?

"Let's get you inside," I said. "You're even more soaked than I am. Come on." I took her arm as I unlocked my door and ushered her in, dropping my purse on the table by the door before heading to the bedroom in search of dry clothes. "Here." I handed her a pair of old sweatpants and a t-shirt. "Put these on while I make us a cup of hot tea. Then tell me what's happened."

Von stripped right there in the living room, looking out the window the whole time, presumably watching for Ben.

"Did he take the truck?" I asked, as I set the water to boil.

She shook her head. "I left it at the nursery in case he comes back to it. Ted brought me home. I filled out a Silver Alert and Ted's taking the deputies back to the nursery to have another look around. They thought I should stay here in case Ben turns up." She pulled the t-shirt over her head and cinched up the pants. I may be just a little bit heavier than Von. "Where could he be, Tabby?" Her voice broke again.

"He just disappeared. One minute he's fertilizing plants, and the next I can't find him anywhere."

"You checked all around here?"

"I did, even in the closets and under the beds, as silly as that might be. Checked the yard and the lot next door, too."

"Have you asked any of the neighbors?"

"Not yet. That's what I was on my way to do when you pulled up. But how could he have even gotten here? The truck is sitting at the nursery right where we parked it this afternoon."

"Why don't you stay here and keep an eye out for him, and I'll go check with the neighbors," I offered, handing her a cup of tea.

"All right. Thank you. That would be a big help. I'm so worried I can't even think straight."

"Do you have your cell?"

"I do. Tried calling him, but he's not answering."

"Call me if he turns up, and I'll call you if any of the neighbors have seen him. Have you called Martha?"

"Not yet," she said. "I don't want to worry her any sooner than I have to."

"What about customers?" I asked. "Would any have seen him?"

"We didn't have very many," she said. "Two or three. Ted took care of them. Nothing out of the ordinary, but I gave the deputies all the information I have. They're going to check video, too, but you know it only shows the entrance. If he wandered off somewhere beyond that, video isn't going to help."

I changed into sneakers and grabbed my umbrella, shaking out the excess water. It had nearly stopped raining, humidity enveloping me as soon as I opened the door. "We'll find him, honey," I said, giving her another hug. "He'll be home before you know it."

I closed the door and sent up a silent prayer, hoping I was right.

An hour later, our little street was hopping with people. Friends and neighbors had all come out to help look for Ben. Ted said it was the same at the nursery, where they'd divided into groups to search surrounding areas. Ben was well-liked by everyone, and I could see it gave Von some measure of comfort to see so many people willing to come out and join the search.

The media, having figured out something was up, came pulling back up to the duplex, piling out of vans and hurrying to set up equipment, calling out to anyone who'd listen, asking what had happened. No doubt they thought Bobby had been in touch somehow, but Von and I decided to take advantage of the opportunity to get word out about Ben. Von was better at that sort of thing than I was, so I let her do all the talking while I stood beside her for support. I wasn't sure how newsworthy local stations would think our situation was, but I hoped they'd at least add something about it to the scrollbar they always have running across the bottom of the television screen these days.

Just as Von was finishing up answering their questions about Ben, her cell phone rang. We stepped away from the cameras as she glanced down at the screen. "Ted," she said, before clicking to answer. I knew if it had just been the two of us, she'd have set it on speaker. As it was, I had to stand there and try to figure out what was going on by watching the expression on Von's face. First, she looked hopeful. Next, she looked confused. Finally, she looked terrified. When it looked like she was going to faint, I took the phone from her hand.

"Tabby here. What's going on? Did you find him?" Von swayed beside me, and I grabbed her arm and led her back to the porch before anyone noticed.

"We haven't found him," Ted answered. "But we found something on the video. Ford F-one-fifty, older model, probably eighty-two. Two-toned, brown and tan. Came in the gate at two-twenty. No passengers, just the driver. Couldn't tell a whole lot, but looked to be a woman, or maybe a smaller man with a ponytail. Left fifteen minutes later with a passenger."

"Was it Ben?" I lowered Von to a porch chair and fanned her with an old magazine while she worked to catch her breath.

"Can't tell. Video isn't clear enough. But that's what the deputies are working on right now. Don't know who else it could have been, if it wasn't Ben."

"So, what, he was *kidnapped*? Is that what you're telling me?"

"They don't know yet, Tabby. All they know is the truck came in with one occupant and left with two, just as the storm clouds were building, right about the time Von started looking for Ben. They're adding the information to the Silver Alert. It'll be all over the place, on the interstate signs and such. We'll find him. Tell that to Von. Truck'll stand out like a sore thumb."

"Now what? We wait for them to find it?"

"People here are still searching, on the off chance it wasn't Ben. That's about all we can do."

"Then that's what we'll do, too," I said. "Call if you find out anything else, and we'll do the same.

Right now, I think I'd better call Martha, Von's daughter, to let her know what's going on. I'd hate for her to see it on the news or flashing on an interstate sign." The same went for Ricky; I'd call him, too, as soon as I finished with Martha.

I'd just hung up and begun scrolling through Von's contacts for Martha's number when the sound of a knocking engine and the smell of exhaust caught my attention. I looked up to see a raggedy-assed old Ford truck creeping down the street, the driver, a young white girl with a ponytail, looking side to side as if searching for an address. Ben sat peacefully in the passenger seat licking an ice cream cone. Vanilla, it looked like, with sprinkles. He waved when he saw Von sitting there on the porch with her mouth hanging open.

Chapter 20: Von

I didn't know whether to kill him or kiss him, to tell you the truth. Him sitting up there in that truck just as happy as could be, licking on that ice cream and waving at me. It seemed like everyone on the whole street fell silent while the girl pulled that wreck of a truck up to my yard and killed the engine before it could die a natural death. She hopped out, ponytail swinging, and ran around to open Ben's door and help him down. When he offered her his arm, I had to restrain myself from yanking the magazine Tabby'd been fanning me with right out of her hand and throwing it at them.

"Ben Powers," I yelled at him, adrenaline pumping through my body hard enough to make me forget about my bad knees as I nearly jumped down the steps to get to him. "What do you think you're doing? You had everybody scared half to death. Where have you been?" I stopped in front of him with my hands fisted on my hips. What I wanted to do was grab him up and kiss him, I was so happy to see him again, even with that big, foolish grin on his face. But I wouldn't let myself do it.

"It's my fault," the girl spoke up. "I'm so sorry. I didn't know. I was looking at the elephant ears, wondering if my yard was too shady for them. I just live down the road, you know. My older brother went to school with Ricky. And Bobby, too, before …" Her eyes flickered toward Tabby. "Well, you know. I'm Mandy." She reached as if to shake my hand. "Mandy Hawkins. My brother's name is Tommy. I'm sure Ricky would remember him."

I remembered Tommy, for sure, and how Tabby had always warned Ricky to stay away from him. Even more clearly than I remembered Tommy, I remembered his older brother Theo. Martha had absolutely hated Theo; more than once I'd had to go up to the high school to talk to the principal after that no-good boy had goosed my girl in the hallway or popped her bra strap in the middle of biology class. The *N* word had been a favorite of his, the *W* word another, and I remember thinking for someone who thought of blacks as *N*s and girls as *W*s, he sure did like putting his hands on them.

Tabby nudged me, and I shook the girl's hand for a second before dropping it to ask, "How in the world did you end up with my husband?"

"That's what I wanted to tell you," she said. "I was looking at the elephant ears and he came up to ask if he could help me. I told him I've always wanted elephant ears along my walkway, but I'm afraid my yard might have too much shade. He offered to take a look at my yard and see. Ordinarily I wouldn't take a man home with me." She stopped, a blush spreading up her neck. "You know what I mean. But since I've always known of y'all and your nursery, there didn't seem to be any harm in it. But then it started storming, and this old truck ain't safe to drive in the rain, bald as the tires are. So I invited him in for a while, until the roads cleared off and I could bring him home. Scared me to death when I saw everyone was looking for him. I'm really sorry; I didn't mean to cause any trouble."

Back in the day, Ben often went with people to offer advice and suggestions on plant choices, so that part wasn't unusual. What was unusual was that Ben climbed up in that girl's truck and took off without letting any of us know where he was going.

"Why would you take off with this girl like that, Ben?"

"How else could I help her but to let her give me a ride? Wasn't like I could drive myself." He licked a drop of ice cream from one knuckle. "You hid my keys from me." A quiet laugh went through the crowd that had gathered around us, and I caught Ben's eye. That man knew *exactly* what he was doing. He was teaching me a lesson, letting me know I couldn't get anything over on him.

"Ben," I started, and then to my horror felt tears coming on.

"Aw, now, honey," he said, stepping forward and putting his arms around me, the ice cream cone falling to the ground. I buried my face in his chest and inhaled his scent, a mix of laundry detergent, bath soap, and a tinge of sweat. I loved that smell, the *Ben-ness* of it. "I shouldn't have done it." He lowered his head to speak into my ear. "I didn't mean to upset you, baby. I just get so angry, feeling like a big ol' seventy-year-old baby. I hate this thing that's happening to me, but I shouldn't take that out on you. I know you're having just as hard a time of it as I am, probably even harder." He snuggled his face into my neck and kissed me, right in the little hollow by my clavicle, where he knew I liked it. "I'm sorry, baby. Forgive me?"

I squeezed him tight, letting his shirt soak up my tears. Around me, I could hear the crowd starting to break up. Pieces of conversation made their way into the strong circle of Ben's arms.

"Glad he's okay …"

"Let them get it sorted out …"

"Poor Von …"

"That old rascal, running off with a pretty young thing …"

I heard Tabby thanking everyone, and the Hawkins girl apologizing again, but I stayed right where I was, where I always wanted to be, until Tabby put her arms around both of us and gently tugged us toward the porch. "Go on," she said, "before y'all embarrass yourselves out here, making out like a couple of teenagers." I felt Ben's laughter rumble in his chest.

"I'll call Martha," she said, "and Ricky, so they won't worry about whatever they might have seen." She pushed the door open. "Well, looky there," she said, as she guided us through our front door. "There's Ricky, now, headed around back. Must have parked down the street to escape all the craziness. I'll go let him in, while you two get reacquainted. Safe sex, now," she said, and my own laughter mixed with Ben's. "We don't want any accidents." She gave us one final little nudge and closed the door softly behind us.

Ben continued holding onto me with one arm,

while with the other he reached to close the blinds. This time, I didn't try to distract him. I knew it was Ben there with me in the dim afternoon light, and even more importantly, he knew it was me. I could see myself reflected in his eyes and knew he was there with me.

Chapter 21: Tabby

I left Von and Ben alone, glad for their reunion, and let myself into my own place, hurrying across the worn kitchen linoleum to let Ricky in through the back. Ricky and I have keys to each other's main doors, of course, but with all the craziness going on I'd latched the storm door, too, and it didn't have an outside lock. It wasn't as if I thought reporters might try to sneak inside, exactly, although I wasn't sure I'd put it past them. It was more that I felt the need to put as many barriers as I could between me and all those camera lenses.

I knew that Ricky, too, preferred to dodge the limelight, which might seem strange, given his profession. But Ricky had always been an observer more than a participant. He was most comfortable standing on the outside and watching other people take center stage. I didn't know if he'd been born that way, or if his childhood had molded him to be that way.

Bobby had always demanded more attention when they were babies, and that didn't stop when he disappeared. Even after I lost him, Bobby continued to dominate my thoughts. After all, I knew how Ricky was doing; I knew he was safe. I could only imagine what might be happening to Bobby, and given what my life with Vern had been like, I didn't imagine it could be anything good. The *unknown* of Bobby's life worried away at me, even in my sleep. There were times I woke up in the dark of night to Ricky patting me on the shoulder saying, "Don't cry, Mom. It'll be okay." I know that's a terrible position to put a child in, but what could I do? That had been our life. It still was; Ricky was still worrying about me, while I worried about his brother.

From the kitchen window, I saw Ricky turn the corner and jog through puddles to the back door, unnoticed by the media. The reporters were back in full force with Ben's arrival, hoping, I suppose, for one last comment from one of us to plaster across live T.V, now that the evening news was on. I could hear the Hawkins girl talking to them through my closed front window. "Oh, sure," she was saying. "I grew up just down the road. I've known these people all my life. I knew Bobby, too. It's crazy about him, isn't it? The way he's showed back up? And the killings, oh, my God. It just goes to show, you never really know who your neighbors are."

I guess she was enjoying her fifteen minutes of fame, as they say. She seemed like a nice enough girl in spite of her primping for the camera. I supposed I could forgive her for that; it isn't every day you're given a shot at an appearance on national T.V. As for me, I couldn't wait for the line of vans to leave our street, something I hoped would happen sooner rather than later. Ben had been found, and my interview with *Swamplands* was coming out in the morning. I couldn't see any reason they'd keep hanging around, and one thing was for certain: as long as the street was packed with reporters, there was no way Bobby could come home. Where in the world was he? Twenty-five years later, and the *unknown* of Bobby's life was still torturing me.

As I stood unlatching the door for Ricky, it hit me that I was still shuffling Ricky aside while I fixated on everything else. I felt terrible about that. The overriding emotion for the majority of my life had been sadness, an overwhelming grief at the loss of Bobby. The second emotion was guilt, because I knew the energy I put into missing one child took away from the energy I put into raising the one right under my nose.

The truth was, Ricky had never asked for much. He'd always been gentle with me; he understood my grief, because he felt it, too. Still, that didn't excuse my neglect; if anything, it made it worse. A prime example: I hadn't taken the time to call him earlier because I'd been dealing with Von, but here he was leaving his job during a week in which he'd already been in trouble with his boss, to rush home again to help me. It was inexcusable, really, the way I always put Ricky last, the way I always knew I could, the way I always knew he'd let me.

I held the door open, an apology already on my lips, when he jumped inside, shaking rainwater from his hair.

That's when I realized.

It wasn't the nearly invisible scar in his hairline caused by a rusty nail during his slide down the shed roof all those years ago.

It wasn't the slightly shaggier haircut from the one

I'd seen on Ricky just that morning.

It wasn't the tiny speck of brown in the middle of all the blue of his right eye.

It was the way the air changed, the energy that always came with him. He'd never been able to enter a room without me knowing, and I knew it then.

Bobby was home.

Chapter 22: Von

I woke up the next morning more full of life than I'd felt in the past year. Ben had come back to me, at least for a few precious hours. I didn't question what the future might hold, because I knew by then there were no promises; I just accepted the blessing of the moment. I won't go into details about our re-union, but I was feeling good that morning, peppy, even, when I woke just before sunrise and put the coffee on.

I pulled my robe tight around me before opening the door, expecting the caravan of reporters to be there as they had the last few days, but the street was quiet, thank goodness, no reporters in sight. The sun was nothing but an orange smear across the sky over to the east when I bent to pick up our copies of *Swamplands*. I was eager to read Tabby's interview, and grateful Ben was sleeping in so Tabby and I could get our coffee and sit out on the porch to read it togeth-er. I gave her front door a soft knock before heading back into my own place to pour the coffee.

Tabby still hadn't shown up by the time I had the coffee poured and muffins on the plate. I supposed she was still sleeping, although, like me, she's typically an early riser. Still, it had been a rough couple of days, and I knew she had to be worn out. We still had nearly two hours before we needed to leave for the nursery, and I considered leaving without her, letting her have the day off, but there just wasn't any way I could do that on a Friday. Fridays were always busy for us, maybe because it was payday for so many folks, or maybe because folks were trying to get a jumpstart on their weekend chores. No, I couldn't give her the whole day, but I could at least give her an extra hour. I folded the paper and stuck it under my purse. I wouldn't read the interview without her; I'd wait until we could both sit down together.

That decision made, I took my muffin and coffee to the living room, turning the T.V. on to catch the morning news. I turned the volume low so as not to disturb Ben, and was just settling into my chair when the phone rang. So much for not waking up Ben, I remember thinking as I struggled to get back on my feet without upsetting my coffee. My heartrate jumped not only from the exertion, but also because a phone call at six o'clock in the morning is rarely a good thing. It wouldn't be Tabby; she'd just knock on the door. And it wouldn't be Martha unless there was an emergency; she wouldn't want to wake up her dad.

When I finally got my legs, robe, and chair cushion untangled enough to make it to the kitchen counter where I'd left my phone, it was Ricky's number I saw on the screen. It wasn't unusual for him to call Tabby early, especially if he knew *Swamplands* was covering a topic she might find interesting. But it *was* unusual for him to call me early in the morning. I fumbled with the button, my fingers always a little clumsy in the mornings, before I finally managed to click the phone to "on."

"Ricky?"

"Yes, ma'am. I'm sorry for calling so early; I hope I didn't wake Uncle Ben, but I'm trying to reach my mom. I know she planned on reading the paper with you as soon as it hit the porch; is she at your place? She isn't answering her phone."

"No," I told him, a little nugget of worry starting to blossom in my chest. "I knocked on her door a while ago, but she didn't answer. I thought she must still be sleeping, it's been such a crazy few days." I was already moving toward the porch. "I'll go knock again. Don't hang up; I'm taking my phone with me."

"Thanks, Aunt Von. I appreciate it. I'm sure she's fine, but I'd feel better knowing."

I stepped out into a morning that was already hot, the sun fully up now, making the air steamy from the previous day's rain. I crossed over to Tabby's door, again giving it a gentle knock, and this time Tabby answered from inside. "Just a minute. Be right there."

"She's here, Ricky. She told me to wait a minute."

"Okay, thank goodness. I'm sure you were right and she was just sleeping. Now I feel guilty for waking her up. Would you just tell her to call me when she gets a chance? I was pretty pleased with the way the interview turned out on paper, but I want to know how she feels about it."

"Sure thing, Ricky. I'll let her know."

"Thanks, Aunt Von." He'd just ended the call when Tabby finally cracked open her door and peeked out.

"Tabby? What's wrong with you? Are you sick? Ricky's been trying to call you, and I knocked on your door half an hour ago. You all right?" I squinted to try and see her better in the dim light of her living room. Funny, for a woman who'd been sleeping in, she looked pretty well put-together. No sleep lines on her face, no mushed-up hair I could see, definitely not the early morning Tabby I'd grown used to. She was fully dressed and apparently ready for work, although as I looked closer, the clothes she wore looked a lot like the ones I'd seen her in the previous afternoon.

"I'm fine, Von, what's all the ruckus about? I've got you knocking, and Ricky calling … Can't a woman bathe in peace around here? All that time in the car has been hard on my back, so I decided to soak in the tub. Tried to, anyway, except I kept getting interrupted." She looked at me over her glasses.

I was torn between feeling sorry for getting her out of the tub, and feeling a little shocked by the dressing down she gave me. Tabby and I didn't usually speak to each other with anger, hadn't, really, since she'd gotten sober, but she sure sounded angry to me just then. "Well, Tabby, last Ricky and I knew, you wanted to read the paper as soon as it hit the porch. Remember? So that's what we were acting on. But I'm sorry we interrupted you. I can see you're busy, so I'll just see you at work. Ricky said to call him when you get a chance."

I turned and went back into my half of the house before she could answer me, closing the door and leaning against it to get my bearings. Tabby wasn't acting like Tabby, which was, of course, a worry to me. The happenings that week would be enough to knock anyone off balance, and with her history, Tabby would always have to be careful. But I hadn't smelled any alcohol and I had a hard time imagining her, after all those years, creeping in the dark of night down to the I-4 overpass that used to be the meeting place for dealers and users. Hell, if nothing else, her knees wouldn't let her meet up at half the places we'd known when we were young and using, a thought that was inappropriately funny at that moment.

I could hear Ben stirring in the bedroom. Pouring out my coffee, now cold, and wrapping up my uneaten breakfast muffin, I tried to put the odd morning out of my thoughts. I wasn't naïve enough to think Ben's clarity of the night before would last through the day, and I knew I'd need all my energy to attend to him and get us both ready for work.

I'd have to worry about Tabby later.

Chapter 23: Tabby

I closed the door, putting my ear against it and listening for Von to leave the porch. At the sound of her own door shutting, I turned back to Bobby, who stood in the shadows behind me, yawning and rubbing his eyes. "That's the first lie I've told Von in years. I can't believe I just did that." I felt sick in the pit of my stomach, but even worse, I felt as if I'd just broken something I might not be able to fix, something very dear to me, and that both hurt and frightened me.

"I know, Mom," Bobby said, moving toward me, "but I just need a few days. Can't I have at least that?" For the briefest of seconds, I moved away from him, my back up against the door. It was involuntary, that step, and I quickly corrected myself, hoping he hadn't noticed.

We'd been up most of the night; I didn't even know when we'd fallen asleep. It was an awkward reunion, nothing like the one I'd spent so many years fantasizing about. There was something invisible, something I can't explain, in the space between us. Something wasn't right, not because I knew Bobby was on the run from the law, and not because he had blood on his hands—literally, under his nails and deep in the creases of his knuckles. I'd seen it when he reached for me as soon as I'd let him in my door. He'd caught my look at the time, glancing down at himself before saying, "Yeah. The rain got most of it off, but not all." It was bizarre, his presence, that comment in my kitchen. But there was something more than that, and the feeling had only grown in the hours we'd spent together.

I've always been a sucker for reunion shows, the ones where the hostess brings together family members who've been separated against their will, or old lovers who never could forget each other. The parent/child reunions were my favorites, for obvious reasons, although it tore me apart to watch them. The host always had one person, usually the parent, sitting on a couch under soft lighting, talking about how much they'd missed their baby and how they'd do anything to find him again.

Then the host would say something like, "We have a little surprise for you," and the audience would gasp because they knew what was coming, even while the parent looked skeptical. Then while everyone's nerves grew tight enough to twang, the music would grow louder, and the missing son or daughter would walk onto the stage from somewhere back in the wings and run over to the parent, who still looked like she couldn't believe it. They'd collapse into each other's arms, sobbing, while the audience sobbed right along with them. While *I* sobbed right along with them, even though I was sitting at home alone on my couch.

They'd hang onto each other and pet each other like they knew each other, even though the reality was they knew each other for maybe ten minutes before the nurse took the baby away, or maybe for a brief few years, like with Bobby and me, before someone else took the child away. I always assumed that's how it would be if Bobby and I ever reunited. He's my *child*, my *baby*, a *part* of me; I've spent most of my life wanting nothing more than to have him back, to hold him again and feel the hole in my heart stitch itself right back up.

But that wasn't how it felt when I first stepped toward him and he wrapped his arms, blood-stained hands and all, around me. It felt awkward, like hugging an unexpected guest much too closely. Like having a stranger touch me in a way that was too personal, a way that felt unnatural and intrusive. Was that what everyone felt, I wondered? When the cameras were off and the host left the stage and the reunited people went home, did they look at each other and wonder, *who is this person?*

Or was it just me? I'd long ago accepted I was different, damaged in some way. Not even all those years of therapy and support groups could erase that knowledge. I could do self-esteem worksheets until the cows came home, but I'd still know, deep within myself, that there was something broken, some healthy, wholesome, human-making ingredient my Higher Power forgot to include when he tossed me together. How else to explain my history? My mother hadn't cared for me at all, dozens of foster parents couldn't deal with me, even my husband had hated me, enough so that he did the one thing he knew might destroy me for good: he took my baby away.

Now that baby was back, and what I felt more than anything in that instant was an absence of everything. I felt numb, and after that, guilty, and after that, afraid, all those feelings flying through me in the time it took to take one small step. Surely that wasn't normal. Surely I was supposed to feel what all those sobbing, wailing mothers felt on T.V. when their middle-aged babies came walking out of the wings. I didn't know what to make of it, didn't know how to explain it to myself, so I did what addicts do: I denied it, just that fast.

I pushed those crazy thoughts out of my head, convincing myself they'd never existed. They became important later on, when I had decisions to make, but at that moment, with my face pressed against Bobby's damp chest while I inhaled the scent of sweat and rain and something else, something foreign to me, I wrapped my arms tight around him and made myself remember the strong-willed little boy I'd grieved for all those years. That gave me something to hold onto. As long as I could keep five-year-old Bobby's face in my mind, I could make thirty-year-old Bobby feel familiar to me. That's when it finally began to hit me that I was holding my baby again, after all, my little freckle-faced rascal, and I might have stood there forever had he not gently pulled back and loosened my arms.

"Shhh," he shushed me. I hadn't known I was making noise until then, the same wailing noise those moms always made on television, and so loud it was bound to carry over to Von's place. "Shhh, Mom," he'd said again, pulling me into the living room and gently pushing me onto the couch. He knelt at my feet. "No one can know I'm here," he said, his voice low. He took my hand, the dirty, slightly sticky feel of his own barely registering before I shoved that thought away, too, and held on tight.

"Bobby," I said, but too many thoughts and questions clogged my throat for me to get any of them out, so I said his name again, the only thing I could say.

"Mom," he said, and reached to touch my cheek with the tips of his fingers. My first instinct was to flinch, that unsettled feeling again, but I closed my eyes and remembered little Bobby, sitting in my lap, patting my cheeks. This was little Bobby. I had to remember that. I opened my eyes to find him staring at me, his expression as confused and pained as my own must have been. "I wouldn't have known you," he said. "We could have passed each other on the street and I don't think I'd have known you."

"I imagine not," I said, trying to smile. "I've aged a bit since the last time you saw me."

"And sobered up," he said, a knife in my heart. "You're sober now, aren't you?"

I nodded, reminding myself that of course he would wonder. His last memories would have been of me slurring my words, gathering him in for a sloppy kiss, passing out on the floor. If he even remembered me at all. If he didn't, I was sure his father had filled his head with enough stories of my failings that he had every right to seem surprised to find me upright and sober. There I was, flinching at my boy's touch while he reached out to me, the addict who'd lost him. What the hell was wrong with me? I didn't deserve the second chance I'd just been given.

"I haven't used since shortly after your father took you," I said.

He looked surprised at that. "That's not what he told me," he said, sitting back on the carpet, peering into my face. "Whenever I'd ask, he said you were either on the streets or in jail. He said Ricky had been taken away from you. Was that true? Did you lose Ricky, too?"

Too? I didn't *lose* you, I wanted to tell him; you were *stolen*. But I held my tongue, because it was all the same. Vern couldn't have stolen Bobby if I'd done a better job keeping up with my children, so he was right, after all. I'd lost him.

"No, I didn't lose Ricky," I said. "He lives just up the road, twenty, thirty minutes from here, depending on traffic. We've been right here all this time, waiting for you to come home."

"I can't believe it," he said, running his hands through hair still moist from the rain, hair just a tad shaggier than Ricky's. The expression on his face was wary. "Dad always said you were gone. Whenever I'd tell him I wanted to go home, he'd say there wasn't a home to go to. He said I was lucky he'd saved me before it was too late."

If Bobby's questioning my sobriety had felt like a knife in my heart, his last words were twisting that knife. I worked to keep my breathing steady; I didn't want him to know he'd hurt me because I wanted him to keep on talking. Besides, I knew, or at least suspected, Vern would have brainwashed him, turning him against me. Still, hearing about it first hand was just about more than I could stand.

All those years I grieved for Bobby, he'd pictured me as a stumbling drunk who'd lost her kids. What hurt more than anything was that it wasn't so far from the truth. I *was* a stumbling drunk when I lost Bobby.

If I hadn't been, maybe I wouldn't have let the boys play all up and down the street the way I did. Maybe I would have heard Ricky hollering and gone to see what was wrong. Maybe I'd have been outside playing with them, instead of three sheets to the wind on the living room floor. The *maybes* had been crushing me to death for years.

But even in the middle of all that, something stood out to me, something I'd been trying to ignore ever since I first saw the news report. "So that's why you never came home? You thought we were gone?"

Bobby nodded. "That's what I'd been told."

"But if you didn't think I was here, what made you come back tonight? How did you know to come?"

"Just a hunch, I guess," he said. "I never could shake this place. You, Ricky. Daddy told me it didn't exist anymore, but I don't think I ever really believed him." He stretched his legs out in front of him, leaning back on his elbows on the floor in front of me, a posture I'd seen Ricky take more times than I could count, especially when he was a teen. It was almost as if the boy had forgotten how to sit up during those years. I wondered if Bobby had done the same, and if Vern had nagged at him the way I'd nagged at Ricky.

"He wanted Ricky, too, you know," Bobby was saying. "But Ricky was hiding. It was his turn; we'd been playing hide-and-seek. When Daddy came by, all he saw was me, so he grabbed me."

Good God, I could have lost them both, was my first thought, one that felt like ice water running down my spine. I wouldn't have survived the loss, of that I had no doubt. I lost half of myself when Bobby was taken; the loss of Ricky would have completely done me in. That bastard, was my second thought. That sorry bastard, may he rot in hell.

And then my third thought: but why? Vern and I had had a rocky relationship, no doubt about it. We were both sick with the disease, both broken kids who'd grown into broken adults. Two broken people, we'd eventually learned, don't add up to one whole one. In the end, the drugs and the fighting took over everything that had ever been good between us, but there *had* been some good between us, in the beginning. We were unhealthy as hell, emotionally speaking, but we were all each other had and we'd done the best we could by each other, until we were so messed up we couldn't.

So why had he had such hatred for me? I'd never knowingly done anything to try to hurt Vern. That isn't to say I never hurt him; I'm sure I did. If you grow up hating yourself, it isn't always easy to show love to someone else. But I hadn't *tried* to hurt him, is what I'm saying. Why had he tried so hard to hurt me? That thought brought up a whole passel of questions I needed to ask Bobby.

"How did you get here?" Out of all the questions I had for him, that was the one that popped out first.

"I caught a ride," he said. "Don't worry about that. The important thing is that I'm here."

He was right, of course, but something about his answer made my initial misgivings flare again. "Bobby, we need to call—"

"No!" he interrupted me. "No phone calls," he said more softly. "No one can know I'm here. Ma, if you're going to call someone, I have to leave, right now. I killed a cop; do you get that? Do you know what they'll do to me when they catch me? Oh, he deserved it, the son of a bitch, no doubt about that, but they don't care about my side of the story. They never do care about us. You know that better than anyone." He reached for my hand again, holding it in both of his. "Just let me stay here," he said, "for a little while, so we can get to know each other again before they take me away."

He was right, I did know that better than anyone, and all I'd wanted forever was to see my son again. There was time, I told myself. I didn't have to make a decision that very moment. We had some time.

"Okay, Bobby," I told him. "Let's not worry about that now. You're right; let's get to know each other again. We'll worry about the rest later."

"Thank you," he said, and laid his head on the couch cushion next to me. "I'm exhausted, Ma. It's been … well, I don't even know how to describe it. What happened with Dad, and everything since. I'm so tired."

My chest constricted as I looked down at him. My poor boy, with all he must have been through. I pushed the hair back from his forehead and was immediately transported back in time. Bobby used to love to have his hair stroked. Some nights it was the only way I could get him to sleep.

"Pretend you're on a cloud," I'd say as I tucked him into bed for the umpteenth time. I'd run my fingers through his hair, gently pushing it off his face, exhaling with relief as his eyes began to close. "Floating above the earth, rocking in the breeze." Visual imagery, a relaxation technique I'd learned from my therapist. It had never worked for me—the booze was faster and more effective—but it had worked for Bobby. "You hear the birds singing," I'd tell him as I smoothed his hair behind his ears and down the back of his neck. "You smell the fresh air. You feel peaceful. Nothing can hurt you on your cloud."

I said the words to Bobby again as my fingers found their way over his scalp, down the back of his neck, feeling the proportions of a grown man with my fingers, but remembering the dimensions of a little boy in my heart.

We sat like that for a long time. I had so many questions to ask, so many thoughts crowding into my head, so much fear crowding into my heart, but none of it could hold a candle to the absolute bliss I felt at having Bobby kneeling beside me, his eyes closed, his body stilled as I stroked his hair. I'd begun to accept I'd never see him again, never have him back, yet here he was. Here we were, together in the quiet night, hidden from everyone, safe, at least for the moment. Nothing could hurt us on our cloud.

At some point, I must have fallen asleep sitting up, my head tilted back against the upholstery. The next thing I knew the phone was ringing, but I was so discombobulated, a feeling that only intensified when I sat up to see Bobby asleep on the floor at my feet, I couldn't remember where I'd put it. By the time I gathered my wits about me, the ringing had stopped.

I glanced at the clock above the television, shocked at the time. Von would be wondering where I was, and Ricky would be expecting to hear from me about the interview. Meanwhile, Bobby was stirring in front of me, sitting up, groaning and rubbing the back of his neck.

"I've got to get ready for work," I said, trying not to panic. "Von'll be here any minute checking on me. I was supposed to have been at her place half an hour ago." No sooner had I said it than there was a knock at the door. Von, I was sure. "Quick, Bobby, go to Ricky's room. Your room," I corrected myself, "while I answer it."

He didn't hesitate, nearly tripping over the coffee table in his haste while I called out to Von to give me just a minute. When I saw him duck into the room he'd shared with Ricky, I cracked open the door to find Von clicking off her phone.

I don't remember exactly what I told her. Something about being in the tub. What I do remember was the look in her eyes. She was hurt by my tone, although she'd never have admitted it. I hadn't meant to hurt her, only to get her to leave. I couldn't let her know Bobby was there. I didn't know exactly what she'd do if she found out, but I had a good idea. Von is a straight-up person. She follows the rules. I couldn't imagine her knowing Bobby was there and not turning him in. So I did what I had to do to keep him safe, just for a little while. Just until we got to know each other again. I lied.

Chapter 24: Von

As if snapping at me and missing our morning coffee hadn't been enough, Tabby was also late for work. The only time I ever remembered Tabby being late was when Ricky was little, when he was sick or had an appointment somewhere. Even then she'd let me know, and I'd be just as worried about Ricky as she was, telling her to call me as soon as she knew anything. That obviously wasn't the case this time, and the alarm bells ringing in my head turned it up a notch.

Thankfully, Ben's good day of the day before had carried over. We'd made it out of the house right on time, and the one lone reporter camped on our street even opened the passenger door for me so I could help Ben in. He teased me on the way to the nursery, making me blush, and took my arm as we walked together to the office. He didn't mention Tabby. He couldn't have known about the events of the morning, but I was a little surprised he didn't ask about her absence.

He headed straight out to get an early start on pruning the jasmine while Ted and I took care of customers. Ben always had preferred working with the plants to working with the people, and there's no end to pruning jasmine in warm weather. I was more than happy to let him do it. I never have liked the stickiness of the cut vines—they'll flat-out ruin your clothes if you aren't dressed for it—although I do love the smell of the flowers.

I was ringing a lady up while Ted loaded her truck with bags of mulch when Tabby finally decided to show up, over an hour late. She'd barely stepped out of her car when she was waylaid by a customer, and I could tell by how quickly she responded to him she was more than happy to put off facing me for as long as she could. I suppose she must have thought I was angry with her, but I wasn't. I'd been a little surprised by the way she'd spoken to me that morning, maybe even a little hurt, but I wasn't angry.

I was worried. The only times I'd known Tabby to stop acting like Tabby, she'd been using. I didn't think she was using again, but I did think something was up. What that *something* might be was worrying me.

I had an idea about it, and I didn't like it at all.

I like to think I'm an intelligent woman. True, my actions haven't always been smart, but I've spent the last three decades getting up and over any roadblocks I put in my own way when I was younger. I've built a marriage, a family, and a business. I've got street sense, common sense, and, after nearly twenty years of piecemealing together a horticulture degree, book sense. All three have served me well, and just then, all three were telling me that Tabby was full of shit.

I stepped from the trailer to wave goodbye to my

customer, and saw Tabby was helping a man pick out some hydrangeas. I hoped she'd remembered to tell him they'd need a lot of afternoon shade. They liked the sun, but *regular* sun and *Florida* sun are two very different things. I'd just started to walk over to them when Ben came up behind me, scaring me half to death, and whispered in my ear, "I see she finally showed up."

"I didn't think you'd noticed," I said, turning to look at him.

"Of course I noticed," he said, swiping a sleeve across his forehead to soak up the sweat. "I noticed she didn't come for coffee this morning, too. What's going on with her, do you think?"

"I hate to say what I'm thinking out loud," I said, and in spite of the topic a shot of pure joy went through me, from my head to my toes. I'd missed this, talking with Ben about everyday happenings, sharing our concerns, gossiping about current events. It was so normal to be standing in the hot Florida sun with my husband, speaking as if nothing had changed, as if we still had all the time in the world to converse. I'd never imagined such a simple pleasure could be taken from us. I'd also never imagined how lonely I would feel when it was. On impulse, I reached around his waist with both arms, and pulled him close to me.

"Careful, woman," he laughed into my hair. "We may have to take an early lunch if you keep this up." He put a finger under my chin and tilted my head, making me look at him. "I love you, Von," he said. "Always have, always will. Remember that on the bad days, when I'm not able to tell you." He leaned down to give me a salty kiss.

"I know you do, baby," I told him, giving him one

last squeeze before letting him go. "And I love you, too. Always have, always will. You remember that on the days you can't hear me say it."

We stood for a minute, side by side, looking out over our nursery as we'd done thousands of times over the years. "I imagine I know what you're thinking," Ben said, picking up our earlier conversation. "You think she's heard from Bobby."

I glanced over to where Tabby was helping the man load plants into his trunk. "It's crossed my mind," I said. "When I left her yesterday she was looking forward to reading the paper this morning, thinking maybe her interview would help Bobby find her, or at least let him know she was still looking for him. Then this morning ..."

"She didn't read the paper," Ben finished for me, "didn't answer the phone when Ricky called, and didn't come for morning coffee. Did the interview not matter anymore when it comes to finding Bobby?"

I didn't answer him. He wasn't expecting an answer, just saying what I'd been thinking, like he always used to do. We watched Tabby lead the man back to the trailer to tally up his total.

"Think about this for a minute, Von. In all the years you've known Tabby, who has always had the ability to make her forget everyone else?"

"Bobby," I answered. It was true. Bobby had always had a way of demanding Tabby's full attention. I'd felt it, and I knew Ricky had felt it.

"Bobby," he agreed.

"She'd take him in if he showed up," I said. "I know she would. She wouldn't think twice about it."

"Do you think he's here?"

"I don't know. I don't *want* to think he's here because what good could come of it? He's running from the police. Even if Vern deserved what he got, and I'm not saying he did, it wasn't Bobby's place to give it to him. But the cops?" I stopped, shaking my head. "That's just pure evil." I shivered. The thought of Bobby next door was enough to make me not want to go home.

"Get those guns, Veronica," Ben said, his voice vibrating low against my ear. "Don't wait on this. Get 'em back today."

Chapter 25: Tabby

I didn't think I'd ever make it to work, there was so much to do, so much to say to Bobby. "I've got to go, Bobby. I wish I didn't, but I can't miss work. Von will definitely know something's up if I do that. Will you be here when I get back?"

"There's nowhere else for me to go."

"All right, then." I couldn't help but notice he hadn't said *I want to be here with you*, or, as he'd said several times the night before, *we need to get to know each other again*. But I let it slide, tamping that little flutter of doubt right back down in my chest as I'd done throughout the night. He was still my child, in spite of what he may or may not have done, and I felt that old familiar pull, the one that had me scheduling conferences with his kindergarten teacher and fighting with old Mr. Wells up the street. I would protect my boy as best I could. I may not have done a good enough job before, but I would now.

There were things I needed to know, but not that morning. That morning, I needed to stick to my routine, to keep Bobby safe. Eventually, I'd have to call the police, but not yet. Not until I'd spent some time with my son and we'd figured out how to get him out of the trouble he'd gotten himself into. I really thought we could, as ignorant as that may sound. I had to believe my son wouldn't have hurt anyone without good reason. It was just a matter of explaining what had happened. He might get some time—I was sure he would—but not life, and certainly not death. We could work with anything less, or at least I could, and I assumed Bobby as well. All of that would have to wait, however. I was already late for work, and there was no way Von would let it slide without demanding some answers.

"Don't open the blinds," I told him. "There's food in the pantry, leftover tuna salad in the refrigerator. Towels are in the hall closet, but you know that. Get whatever you need. Make yourself at home." I cringed at that last one. It *was* his home, wasn't it? Did the fact he'd been taken from it mean it was no longer his?

"I got it, Ma," he said. "I just want a shower and some sleep. Maybe some food, if I'm not too tired to eat. It's been a hell of a couple of days."

"Bobby," I said, gathering my purse, pulling out my keys. "Be careful, okay? Just sit tight until we can get all this figured out."

"I'll be fine," he said, stepping toward me and folding me into a hug. "I'll be here when you get home." I hugged him back until I had to let go before tearing up again.

I let myself out, making sure to lock the door behind me. I didn't know how I'd explain my lateness to Von, especially after missing the paper and coffee over at her place. It didn't feel right, having a distance between us. I needed her to forgive me, but how could she do that when I couldn't explain what was wrong?

Luckily, no sooner had I stepped out of the car than a customer approached me, and that was pretty much the way the entire morning went. It was easy enough to avoid Von, although I felt terrible doing it. When I did find myself face-to-face with her, I tried to be extra nice. I lifted plants, swept the office, answered the phone, and did everything else I could think of to try to make things up to her, but of course I couldn't. The only way to make things up to Von was to be honest with her, and that was impossible.

She knew, though. Von always knows.

Ricky called just before lunch to ask where I'd been and what I'd thought of the article. "I overslept this morning," I told him, not exactly the whole truth, but not exactly a lie, either. "I thought he did a good job, though, didn't you?" My second lie of the day was surprisingly easy. I hadn't read the article yet. I hadn't had a chance, but I was hoping if there'd been an issue with it, Ricky would have been more persistent in trying to reach me, to warn me. My instinct paid off.

"I thought he was fair," Ricky answered. "But I don't think that's the end of it."

"What do you mean?" I absentmindedly plucked a caterpillar from an oleander plant, my thoughts splintered in too many directions to concentrate fully on what he was saying.

"I mean this is *Swamplands*," he replied, "and they'll do whatever they need to do to keep the online clicks coming. There are some rumors floating around."

"What kind of rumors?"

"I'd rather talk about it in person," he said. "I should get out of here on time today, so I can be at the duplex by six. Don't cook; we'll order something. Love you, Ma," he said, "but I've got to run. I need to meet with Gerry about a story he's doing. See you this evening."

He was gone before I could respond. I slipped the phone into my pocket and turned to find Von looking at me.

She has a particular way of standing, Von does, when she wants you to know she's not pleased. Feet spread shoulder-width apart, she places her hands on her hips, but not the way most folks do. Von rests the backs of her hands on her hips and stands square in front of you, legs braced, looking you up and down, her lips pursed out, forehead bunched up like it does when she's mad. She doesn't say anything, just stands there with that look. I've seen her use it on her kid, my kids, Ben, and even on customers if she thinks they're being particularly difficult and unreasonable. She also uses it on me, although I hadn't been the recipient of it in years.

"What?" I asked, taking a step back. I wasn't afraid of Von, of course, but she has a powerful presence when she's angry.

"I need the guns back," she said.

"What? Why?" I don't know what I'd been expecting her to say, but that wasn't it.

She stood there a few seconds, looking me up and down again before answering. "I have never lied to you," she said, "and I won't start now, although I'm willing to bet you can't say the same."

I opened my mouth to protest—God only knows

what I could have said—but she cut me off before I started.

"I believe you've heard from Bobby. Don't even start," she said when I opened my mouth again. "I've known you at your best, Tabby, but I've also known you at your worst and every stage in between. I don't want to hear any lies, so I'm not going to put you in the position to have to lie. Don't tell me anything. Just give them back."

"But what about Ben?" I asked. Von had come to me toting a long, narrow, incredibly heavy plastic box shortly after Ben's symptoms became undeniable. It was one of those under-the-bed boxes you can find at any Wal-Mart or Family Dollar store, the kind people use to pack away winter clothes during summer or some such thing. I'd shoved it under my bed, right next to the small lockbox that holds my own pistol, a .38 snub nose revolver Ben brought me shortly after Bobby was taken. I didn't know where he'd gotten it and I didn't ask, but I sure was grateful to have it. I was afraid, back then—terrified, actually—that Vern would come back and steal Ricky, too. Without a doubt, I'd have killed him if he'd tried.

"Not the most accurate," he'd told me at the time, "but it'll get the job done, if needed. Keep it locked up where Ricky can't get to it." I had, all the way until Ricky was grown and gone. Several times since he'd moved out I'd thought of returning it to Ben. I no longer lived in fear of Vern returning to steal Ricky. Now my fears of something happening to Ricky centered on the terrible traffic on I-4, or some of the crime-ridden areas he sometimes had to visit to get his stories. Eventually I forgot about the pistol, and then Von had shown up asking me to keep Ben's, as well, which put an end to any thought I'd had of giving mine back to him. Now here she was asking me to return them.

"Ben would never hurt anyone," she said, in answer to my question. "I was afraid he'd hurt himself, that he'd forget how to load one or clean one in the middle of doing it, and end up hurting himself. I'll just have to make sure that doesn't happen. I can do that. What I can't do is control what happens at your place, especially when I don't even know for sure what's going on over there. So we need to get those guns back."

"I'm sorry, Von," I said. I couldn't explain further; I could only hope she understood.

"I know," she said, nodding, "but don't forget Ricky."

"What do you mean?"

"I mean that boy has come second his entire life, both when Bobby was here, and when he wasn't. You make sure Ricky comes first this time."

The truth of her words hurt. Here I'd already gone and ignored Ricky's call, forgotten to call him back, and lied to him—one-and-a-half lies, actually—within the space of a few seconds. But what else could I have done? Even as those thoughts bounced around in my head, a part of me was trying to figure out how to hide Bobby when Ricky came for dinner.

"I need to go home for lunch," I said, and if Von was surprised by the sudden change of topic, she didn't show it.

"Try to be back on time," she said, and my face burned with shame.

"Von, you know I'm never late. This morning was just … I was …" I sighed. "I'll be back in time," I told her. "I promise."

She didn't answer me, just turned and walked back through the oleanders to the office.

I was so frazzled and upset by everything happening I barely even remember the drive home. What I do remember, and wish I didn't, was the sight of Bobby naked on my living room floor, pounding away into the equally naked Hawkins girl.

Chapter 26: Ricky

W hat the hell, Gerry? Why would you do this?" I was so angry I couldn't see straight. As it turned out, I'd had to work late the day before because Gerry was on special assignment, covering me. And Mom. The resultant article was a field day of speculation, sensationalism, and mudslinging. Unfortunately, some of it was also official. He'd found old child welfare records I hadn't even known existed. The details were graphic and damning. Some of it I'd known, but much of it I hadn't. So much for confidentiality. I supposed anyone was amenable to temptation, if the price was high enough.

It didn't hurt me—I didn't care what people thought of me, and I knew my mother loved me—but I also knew my mother, an avid reader of *Swamplands*, would be mortified. "What about my mom?" I asked. "Can you imagine how she'll feel reading this?"

Gerry shrugged. "It's the job, man. Andy sent me to get him a story, so that's what I did."

"Seriously? You're okay with this?"

Another shrug. "Look, man. I tried to talk to you, but you didn't have time. Shoved me into a wall, if I remember right. And I had a deadline, so I met it." I could only stare after him as he sauntered down the hall. I briefly toyed with going after him, demonstrating that my offhand nudge the day before was in no way indicative of what I *could* do, if pushed. Before I could make up my mind, my cell rang. Glancing down, I saw it was Aunt Von. I'd spoken to Mom only moments before; I wondered what in the world Aunt Von might need.

"What's up?" I asked, working hard to sound nonchalant.

"It's me, Ricky," said Uncle Ben.

I was stunned. Uncle Ben didn't make phone calls, even before the Alzheimer's. "Hey, Von," he'd yell. "Could you call Pope's Garage for me? I need to check on that alternator." The man had always hated talking on the phone. The fact that he was on the other end of it quite honestly scared the crap out of me.

"Uncle Ben? Is everything okay?"

"Well, now," he said, "I reckon that depends on your definition. Everyone is alive, if that's what you mean."

I nearly smiled at Uncle Ben's cadence, until his next words.

"Von and me, we think your mom has heard from Bobby."

"What makes you think that?" I asked, immediately on alert.

"I don't want to go into all of it. Don't have time, anyhow. Your mom'll be back from lunch any minute and she doesn't know I'm calling you. Von's out there to distract her if she gets back too soon, although 'too soon' doesn't seem to be a problem with Tabby this morning."

"What do you mean?"

"I mean she was late to work. Real late."

"Mom's never late to work."

"I know. That's what I'm trying to tell you. Something's going on, Ricky. I heard she didn't answer your call this morning, and she never did come for coffee with Von. Then showed up almost two hours late to work. Won't even look Von in the eye. We think she has him."

"Has him? What do you mean, 'has him'?"

"I mean I think she's hiding Bobby right next door."

"Shit."

"Mind your language, boy. Smart minds think of better words."

I did laugh at that, in spite of my anxiety. Uncle Ben never was one for letting me curse, even if he did let a few slip himself. "Uncle Ben, how could Bobby have possibly gotten to my mom with all the traffic around there these days? You know the sheriff's department is patrolling the street, plus all those reporters, not to mention all the people out looking for you when you went missing."

"Damn, boy," Uncle Ben said, apparently forgetting that smart minds could think of better words. "Wasn't missing, just wasn't where Von expected me to be. Sometimes I get so damned tired of people fussing over me and thinking they need to know every move I make, every thought in my head."

"I realize that," I said, eager to get him back on track. "I know it sucks. I'm sorry, Uncle Ben. But about Bobby, with all that going on, how could he have shown up at Mom's?"

"Maybe that's exactly how he did it," said Uncle Ben. "Maybe there was so much craziness going on he managed to slip right through."

Maybe, but I wasn't convinced. It seemed a long leap to me to assume that just because my mother was acting weird, she was hiding Bobby. "Well, I'm going to her place for dinner tonight," I told Uncle Ben. "If Bobby's there, it'll be hard for her to hide him." Our half of the duplex was just a little over 1,200 square feet. It had never seemed crowded to us, but it certainly wasn't big enough to hide a grown man.

"Be careful, Ricky," Uncle Ben said. "Holler if you need us; we'll be right next door. And keep your eyes and ears open." He paused for a few seconds, and I could hear him breathing into the mouthpiece. "Son, you know if he's there, we're going to have to call the sheriff's office."

"I'll be the first one to call them if I see anything strange, Uncle Ben," I promised. If my mother was indeed hiding Bobby—and I didn't believe she was, not for a minute—it could lead to nothing but trouble for her. As terrible as it would be for me to turn in my own brother, my first responsibility was to my mother. I had to protect her, not so much from Bobby, but from herself.

Even knowing Bobby had killed our father, I couldn't imagine him hurting our mother. Given the few memories I had of Vern, I could envision a situation in which Bobby had to defend himself, at the cost of my father's life. Maybe all those years with my father had damaged him in some way, had brought out a cruelty that may have otherwise remained untapped. I couldn't explain his actions, but I also couldn't imagine Bobby ever wanting to hurt our mother, because in spite of everything, her love for us had always shone through. Having said that, I knew my mother well enough to know she'd sacrifice everything to protect him, even her own freedom. I wouldn't let her do that, even if it meant quite literally turning in my other half.

Uncle Ben terminated our call with instructions to let him know what I found at my mother's place, and I clicked off the phone and sat at my desk, rendered nearly catatonic by a flood of emotions. I've always been a methodical person, but as I struggled to categorize the thoughts and feelings overwhelming me, I found it was impossible to do. Much of what I felt was indefinable, and my thoughts had nowhere to go other than in circles.

The events of the past couple of days had happened so quickly I'd barely had time to process any of it. I'd lurched from one event to the next, taking Mom to Tampa, doing damage control at work, learning Uncle Ben had disappeared, stumbling across Gerry's damning *Swamplands* article, and now this. What I'd successfully managed to do, during the chaos, was to avoid examining my own feelings regarding Bobby's reappearance.

The truth of the matter was, I didn't know how I felt about not only his reappearance, but about Bobby in general. I'd been so young when he was taken I had very few memories of him, and those memories were, at best, mixed. I remembered having a constant playmate, but I also remembered being an anxious little kid, worried about pleasing Bobby or making sure I got my fair share of whatever it was we happened to be fighting over at the moment, whether that was attention or the last cookie in the jar.

We were identical twins, and although I spent a good portion of my late teens and early twenties researching the mysterious bond supposedly shared by identical twins, I couldn't say with any sort of conviction I *felt* that bond. How would I know? It's like asking a colorblind man what the color *red* looks like to him. How can a person describe something they don't know? When Bobby was taken what I felt more than anything was confusion. Why did Daddy come and get Bobby, but not me? Once I saw the reaction of the adults in my life, I felt fear. Daddy driving off with Bobby was a *bad* thing, I came to understand.

But when you're five years old, events around you are understood in an egocentric sort of way. I couldn't, back then, understand what Bobby's abduction meant in any larger sense. I didn't think of things in terms of, "Wow, this is really going to change our lives." I thought in terms of, "I wish Mommy would stop crying and take me to the park." I understood that the adults around me were sad and angry, but I also enjoyed the extra attention I received from Aunt Von and Uncle Ben.

I don't know how old I was when I finally understood the ramifications of his disappearance. I do know it didn't happen all at once. At some point, I began to understand he wasn't coming back, even though the thought was inconceivable to me. Bobby had always been with me; how could he not be? I became afraid of the dark, and afraid of being alone. I grew to understand that Mom had changed, and that the change was permanent. There would be no more carefree days at the beach with my beautiful stranger-mom in her purple bathing suit. There would be no more carefree days, period. In the following years Mom would laugh again, but never fully, nothing like the deep belly laugh I'd always loved. If I'd felt in my earliest years that Bobby somehow came first in our inevitable sibling rivalry while he was with us, I knew it as fact after he disappeared.

Given all that, I didn't know how to feel about his unexpected return. What I did know was this: I had to protect my mother, and she would not make it easy for me.

Chapter 27: Tabby

I waited if not patiently, at least quietly while Bobby and the Hawkins girl scrambled to get their clothes on. I stared at the floor, carefully avoiding looking at either of them, until she finally grabbed her purse and let herself out the back door, blouse buttoned crooked and pink bra crumpled in one hand, with a kiss blown to Bobby but not a word spoken to me, which was just as well. I watched her for a moment as she darted across the backyard and disappeared into the undeveloped land behind us. Then, in the hot afternoon sunlight filtered by our closed window blinds, as dust motes danced in the air and a mockingbird called somewhere outside, I turned to Bobby.

"You know her," I said, standing in the same spot I'd stood since finding them in the living room floor.

He nodded, his face still flushed. "For a few years now."

My mouth dropped open in surprise. "How?"

"I remember her," he said. "She was in kindergarten with me and Ricky."

I shook my head, confused. I had no idea how to handle the situation. I couldn't be angry with Bobby for having sex with a neighbor. He was thirty years old, after all. I never asked after Ricky's sex life. Never wanted to know, and assumed he'd tell me if there was anything important enough to tell. But Bobby, in my living room, while on the run from police, after having been missing for years, with a girl who lived just around the corner. It was all too much. I had no idea how to react.

"Look, Ma," he said. "I …" He stopped, sinking into the couch and scrubbing a hand through his hair. His belt still dangled unfastened, jingling as he moved, and a swatch of plaid underwear stuck out of his fly. I had to look away again.

"I haven't been completely honest with you. I've kept up with you the last few years. You and Ricky both. I've been back here a few times. Just wait," he said, when I tried to interrupt, stunned at what I was hearing.

"I've driven by," he went on, in spite of my sputtering. "Walked the neighborhood. After we moved back to Tampa, I mean. It was during one of those first trips I met Mandy. Or re-met, I guess I should say, because I really did remember her. She used to follow Ricky around like a little lost puppy. When I first saw her again, she was walking down the road in a bathing suit, no shoes, swinging a gas can. The gas gauge in her truck is broken, and she's forever running out of gas. She's not the sharpest knife in the drawer, but she's got a killer body."

"You've been here." I repeated what he'd said, trying to let it sink in.

"A few times," he said. "Quite a few, actually, mostly after Mandy and I hooked up."

"Mandy." I couldn't seem to keep from echoing him. "She helped you escape." It wasn't a question; things were becoming clear to me now.

"And distracted the reporters and everyone else by talking Uncle Ben into leaving the nursery with her," he confirmed.

"You had it all planned out."

"Well, of course. I said *she* was stupid; I didn't say *I* was."

"Did you ever stop to think how Von might feel? She was scared to death, Bobby. We all were."

"Oh, come on. Ben had a blast. He got to spend time with a hot chick, got to eat ice cream, and at the same time, got to stick it to all y'all who keep tabs on him like he's some kind of retard. If anything, we did him a favor. And I got to come home. It was the only way I could get here. Doesn't that make it worth it?"

How could I argue with that? As much as I hated what Von had gone through, and as much as I, too, had worried about Ben, having Bobby home was everything to me. No cost was too great, but his recklessness frightened me.

"Don't you think the police are watching her?" I asked. "If they know she's your girlfriend—"

"They don't," he said, hooking his hands behind his head with a loud sigh. "And she's not. She's more of a friend with benefits. A fuck buddy."

I winced. I hated that word. It had been one of Vern's favorites; he'd used it as literally every part of speech. There were certain words Ricky had known not to use around me, and Bobby had just used two of them in as many minutes. But of course, Bobby didn't know my house rules, and I doubted very much Vern had had any.

"We'd hook up whenever I came to town," he said, "but no one knew. Her brother saw us once, but he just assumed I was Ricky, so we let him run with that idea. I did a hell of a good impression, if I do say so myself, especially for someone who hasn't even spoken to Ricky in decades. It was freakin' hilarious. Mandy said the only thing wrong with my impression was that if I was really Ricky, I'd be too damned conceited to ever be with her in the first place."

"Bobby." I glanced over at him, trying to capture what he was saying, attempting to gather it up and arrange it into some sort of order that might make sense, but it was impossible, like trying to collect dandelion fluff and put it back in place. "Who are you?" I asked, meaning all of it, everything. *Who* are *you, for God's sake?*

"We lived in Minnesota for a while," he said, as if he'd understood my question and was attempting to answer it. "Lots of snow, is what I remember most. At first it was fun, seeing snow for the first time. But then it was just cold. Dirty, gray, all the snow shoved over to the sides of the roads for months on end, pissed on by dogs, full of garbage, and piled up higher than my head until it finally melted mid-summer. Then North Dakota, Montana, Washington, Oregon.

"Everywhere, really, or at least everywhere we could go that was far enough away from Florida. But all the places were the same, because we always stayed in the same sort of place. The sort of places people like us stay. White trash is still trash, no matter where you go, right?" He didn't wait for an answer. "Dad picked up work, construction, landscaping, that sort of thing. Never enough money for food, school supplies, clothes. But always enough for booze. Gotta have priorities, know what I mean?"

I stood quietly with my arms wrapped around myself, trying to hold the pieces of my heart together. They seemed to slide around in my chest like slivers of broken glass. I could feel his anger, directed at both his father and me. What had I done, bringing this child into that sort of life? I ached for him, for the things he'd experienced. I'd spent the many years of his disappearance drowning in guilt caused by my own failings, but never more so than at that moment.

"We moved a couple of times a year, whenever Dad would get fired," he said. "We used fake names. I grew up as Timmy. Timmy Clay. Close, right? But different enough to avoid suspicion. Hell, after enough years, that name was more familiar to me than the one you gave me. I think of myself as Timmy, not Bobby. You want to know who I am? That's who I am. Timmy Clay." If he saw me flinch, he ignored it.

"Sometimes he enrolled me in school," he said, "sometimes not, if he was paranoid. Told anyone who asked that he was homeschooling. Didn't want to leave any sort of trail, you know. Nothing that could give us away. I guess in a way he *was* homeschooling, just not in any subjects that were likely to set me on the right path, if you know what I mean.

"Anyway, I dropped out as soon as I could, when I turned sixteen and found out I was going to have to repeat ninth grade again. We were back in Montana by then, so it was legal. I'd have quit sooner but Dad didn't want any truant officers coming after us, so I waited. Not much point going to school, though, if you never learn anything, and it's hard to learn anything when you live the way we did."

I pulled a chair from the kitchen table and dragged it to the living room where I sat, facing him, giving us both our space. The barred shadows of the window blinds fell across his face, making it impossible to read his expression. I shivered, seeing the bars of a jail cell in place of shadows. I didn't want to think about that.

"Go on," I said. "I'm listening." I was afraid of interrupting him, afraid he'd fall silent and leave my questions unanswered, but he didn't.

"We did that, lived that way, until I was eighteen," he said. "And then we came back to Florida."

"Tampa," I said, and he nodded.

"I guess when I turned eighteen Dad figured there was no more reason to run," he said. "No more reason to hide me. He'd always missed Florida. He hated the cold, but you probably know that."

I didn't. I'd never lived anywhere but Florida, and neither had Vern, back when I'd known him. I kept quiet, waiting for Bobby to speak again.

"That's when I started coming back here." He shrugged, letting his hands fall into his lap.

"But why—"

"Why didn't I come home?" He interrupted me before I could ask. "At first it was because I didn't even know if you were still here. Then once, I saw Ricky. He was playing basketball in the driveway with some other kids. And he looked okay, you know? I mean, he looked *good*. Normal. Happy. Like a high school senior *should* look. After that, I was afraid to come home."

"Bobby, *why*? When I think that all this time, I could have … you could have been here, with me. With us. All I ever wanted was to have you back. That's all I've been able to think about since you disappeared. I don't understand." The glass shards in my chest shifted position and I nearly gasped aloud.

"You all looked so happy," he said. "You and Ricky, Aunt Von and Uncle Ben. You had such normal lives. I was afraid there wasn't a place for me."

"My God, Bobby. Surely you must know how I looked for you. We all did. We never stopped. Not a day has gone by that I haven't tried to figure out how to find you and bring you home."

"How could I have known?" he asked. "Dad sure as hell didn't tell me. For all I knew, you were living on the streets and Ricky was lost somewhere in the system. When we moved back to Florida and I realized you were still here, in this very house, it seemed to me like you all had done just fine without me. You guys had moved on; there wasn't any way to go back."

"No, Bobby." I crossed the space between us and knelt in front of him, taking his face in my hands and pulling him close, forehead to forehead. "Look at me. We weren't okay. We hadn't moved on. There's been a massive hole in our lives, in our hearts, since you were taken from us. I got up every damned day and put one foot in front of the other because I had to. I still had to take care of Ricky. But I've been a broken person since your dad took you away."

"Well, I'm here now." He reached up to remove my hands from his face and stood, knocking me over backwards in his apparent hurry to get away from me.

"Can you honestly say you're happy about that?" There was an edge to his voice.

I scrambled to get up. "Of course I'm happy. What are you talking about? Bobby—"

"Do you think I haven't seen the way you flinch when I get too close? The way you stiffen up when I hug you? You always thought you were so slick, able to hide things from other people. But you aren't. You never were. I know exactly how you feel about me."

Before I could answer, my cell phone rang with a chime reserved for Von. I glanced over to where I'd dropped my purse on the end table when I'd first walked in.

"Saved by the bell," said Bobby. "Better answer it. You wouldn't want to raise suspicion." I was frustrated at the interruption, but the phone was still ringing and he was right. I didn't want to raise suspicion.

"Von," I said by way of greeting. "I'm coming. I still have a few minutes."

"So you do," she said, "but that's not why I'm calling. Ben wants you to bring those guns back with you." She was all business, her words clipped and direct.

"Okay," I answered. "I'll put them in my trunk. But wouldn't it be easier for me to just bring them over when you get home?"

"We've been talking about it, and Ben doesn't want to wait," she said. "Neither do I."

I struggled to keep my voice light. "Well, that doesn't make any sense to me," I said, "but whatever. I'll load them up right now."

"I appreciate it," she said, before disconnecting.

I didn't want to leave Bobby, but I didn't have much choice, not if I wanted to keep up any appearance of normality. Besides, I could hear the water running in the bathroom down the hall, so it appeared he'd decided he had enough of me for the time being, anyway. I propped open the front door and popped the lid to my trunk, then went down the hall to my bedroom.

Kneeling on the floor, I pulled the box from under the bed, struggling with the weight of it. I unclipped the lid to make sure everything was as it should be, and then, as an afterthought, stretched to reach the lockbox that housed my .38. I worked the combination lock, retrieved my revolver, and slid the empty lockbox back to its place under the bed. Quickly, I rearranged Ben's arsenal in order to fit the pistol in, then snapped the lid closed again.

I don't know what made me do that.

I swear to God, I don't.

I had just regained my feet, struggling to balance the heavy box in my arms, when Bobby's voice came from behind me.

"Getting rid of the guns, huh?"

"What? How did you …?" I turned to look at him. He was shirtless, his belt still dangling, holding a toothbrush in one hand, a towel in the other.

"I had a look around this morning," he said, one side of his mouth twerked up in a smile that reminded me of his childhood, except that when he was a child, I'd never startled at his presence the way I did now. "You won't want to forget these." He reached up into my closet, deep behind a stack of folded quilts, and retrieved a box of ammunition, unlatching the box lid and tossing it inside. Surprised, I stumbled backwards under the added weight.

"I hope you don't mind," he said, "but I found some extra toothbrushes and stuff under the bathroom sink, and some clothes in our old closet. I assume they're Ricky's, but they fit me perfectly. I'd like to take a shower now. Actually, I would have liked to have taken one earlier, but Mandy didn't want to wait."

"Of course," I said, finally finding my voice. My arms were beginning to tremble from the weight of the box and I shifted it, nearly dropping it in the process. "Use whatever you need."

"Everything but the guns?" he asked. "Relax, Ma. I'm joking. Let me give you a hand with that." He reached to take the box from me. "Where are you taking them?"

"To the car," I said. "Ben wants me to bring them back to the nursery with me."

"He does, huh? Wild animals eating the plants? Deer, maybe? Rabbits?"

"They're his," I said. "Von was just keeping them here because Ben had a bad spell. He has Alzheimer's—"

"You don't need to explain. Just hand them over."

He reached for the box again. I held onto it just a fraction too long, another detail he noticed if his raised brow was any indication, before letting go and handing it over with relief. I followed him down the hall, rubbing the circulation back into my arms. Bobby or no Bobby, I suddenly felt desperate for fresh air and sunshine, the cramped duplex closing in around me and making it difficult to think.

He stopped so suddenly in front of me I nearly ran into the back of him. "Here you go," he said, turning to hand the guns back to me while, to my complete surprise, he planted a kiss on the top of my head.

"Sorry about getting angry," he said. "I know it's awkward, for both of us. I have a lot to sort out. I don't know what was true, and what wasn't. I have to rethink everything I thought I knew. It's going to take some time."

I wanted to pull him into my arms and reassure him, but that damned box prevented me from doing it. "Bobby," I said through sudden tears. "I'm so glad you're back. We'll get this figured out, okay? Trust me. All that matters is that you're here."

"Sure, Ma," he said, sidestepping into the shadows as I approached the door. "I trust you." Was he mocking me? It was impossible to sort out what was resentment on Bobby's part, and guilt on mine. Everything was distorted, filtered through so many layers of memories and emotions I couldn't figure out what was real.

The box safely stowed away in the trunk, I'd just turned back to close and lock the door to the duplex when I remembered. "Bobby," I called out softly, and he peered around the frame of the bathroom door. "Ricky is coming for dinner tonight. I can't tell him not to come. Maybe we should tell him—"

"No," he said, moving toward me down the hall. "No one can know. Not even Ricky."

We needed to let Ricky know what was going on. He had a right to know. But I didn't want to argue with Bobby, and didn't have time, anyway. We'd have to figure it out later.

"Have him over," he said. "It'll be good to see him, even if he doesn't see me. I'll hide. I've gotten good at it over the years." That half-smile again.

"For God's sake, relax" he said again, with a roll of his eyes. It was such a Ricky-like gesture it was almost possible to think Bobby had never been gone. Had, in fact, been there all along, rolling his eyes and sighing right along with Ricky whenever I did something to annoy him. Then he was gone, disappearing back into the bathroom.

I started for the car before hesitating. Popping open the trunk again, I opened the box and retrieved my .38. Slamming the trunk closed and circling back to the driver's side, I slid in and closed the door, sweating in the trapped heat. I pushed the button and clicked open the revolver. Four bullets. I had the vaguest of memories: a shooting range with Ben. "Empty it before you store it," he'd said. "You don't need a loaded gun around with Ricky into everything. Clean it, too. If you don't take care of it, it won't take care of you."

But I'd done neither. It had been late in the day, time to start dinner, and besides, if Vern showed back up to steal Ricky away, too, what good was an empty gun? So I'd stored it back in the lockbox as it was, and there it had been for over twenty years.

I rotated it, closed it, and slid it under the driver's seat, deep between the rails.

Chapter 28: Ricky

The change in my mother was concerning. When I'd seen her just the day before she'd been, if frazzled, at least hopeful, a look I'd barely recognized. But now, when I turned off the engine and she met me at the door, she looked as if she'd aged a decade in the last twenty-four hours. She had dark circles under her eyes and the faint lines bracketing her mouth looked deeper, more downturned.

Maybe Uncle Ben was right. *Something* had certainly happened.

"Ricky, you didn't have to," she said, taking the bucket of chicken out of my hands as I leaned over to kiss her cheek. "I could have thrown something together for us."

"No need," I said. "Besides, you don't know the secret recipe." I glanced sideways at her, hoping for a smile at my lame joke, but no such luck. "Are you okay?" I asked, following her inside and reaching into the cabinet for a couple of plates. A quick look around showed nothing out of place. If Bobby was there, he was doing a good job hiding. "You don't seem like yourself." I studied her expression, even more concerned by the pallor of her skin under the kitchen's florescent bulb.

"Oh." She hesitated. "I'm fine, honey. Just, you know. Tired. A little stressed. It's been a weird week, hasn't it? I'm not quite sure how to handle it all."

"It has." It was my turn to hesitate. I set the table and poured tea before deciding it would do more harm than good to avoid telling her about Gerry's article. "Ready?" I pulled out her chair before taking my own. "I hate to even mention this," I said, toying with my fork, "but I'm afraid it's about to get even more stressful."

She went still, her tea glass halfway to her mouth. "What do you mean?"

I cleared my throat. "A couple of things. First, the second cop, the one in intensive care? It's bad, Mom. Doesn't look like he's going to make it, and even if he does, he's suffered a massive traumatic brain injury."

She placed a hand over her eyes, as if she could block out what I'd just said. "Dear God." After a moment, I could see her willing herself to sit up straight and look at me. She squared her shoulders and took a deep breath. "What else?"

As always, I marveled at my mother's toughness. She'd been through hell and back in her lifetime, but she'd always managed to come out in one piece. Battered, maybe, and bruised, but intact. She was the strongest woman I'd ever known. Still, we were swimming in uncharted waters, and I worried about her. "It's Gerry," I said. "You know how Andy is, always sending someone out to find 'the story under the story.' Well, Andy sent Gerry out to find the story under *our* story."

The relief on her face was evident. "I'm not worried about that," she said, stabbing at her potato salad. "After all, we already talked to Andy about all of it. What else is there to say?"

"He uncovered old records from the Department. Child welfare records."

Her face drained of color. "You mean he bribed someone," she said, pushing her plate away. "Those records are confidential, Ricky. He shouldn't be able to get to them."

"He shouldn't, but he did," I answered. "Bribed is probably the right word. Look, Mom, you know I don't care about any of it. I know how much you love us. But he's pissed at me—long story—so he's going to make it as ugly as he can. He'll make an argument that it was Bobby's messed up childhood—that it was your parenting," I clarified, "that led to the death of one cop, and very possibly two. He's even interviewed a local psychologist about the importance of healthy parent-child bonding in the early formative years. Apparently, the guy is an expert in the study of attachment disorders."

"Of course he is," she said bitterly, tossing her napkin on top of the untouched plate. "Goddamned experts. What are they good for, other than spouting off nonsensical bullshit and making up ridiculous syndromes and disorders? Not a goddamned one of them ever helped me."

I let her vent. I couldn't very well argue, since, for the most part, I agreed with her. When she quieted down, I pressed on. "You and I know better," I said, "but that's the angle he's going to take. It's all about web traffic, and the more shocking, the better."

She dropped her head to her hands, elbows propped on the table, seemingly spent. "There's just no end, is there? It doesn't matter how hard you work to make up for your mistakes, you never really can. They're still there, just waiting to bite you in the ass the first chance they get. It *is* my fault, Ricky. That's the thing. There's no getting around it."

"That's not true, Mom. Whatever mistakes you made, you fixed a long time ago. You're not responsible for whatever Bobby may or may not have done."

She just shook her head.

"Do you want the specifics of what he found?" I asked. "Or would you rather not know?"

"I don't know. Do I want the specifics? Do I need to hear them? So much of it is burned into my brain, but there are other parts—you know this, Ricky—I was so wasted I barely remember a thing."

"Those are the parts he's focused on."

She took a deep breath and sat up in her chair. "Lay it on me," she said. "I might as well know."

"There was something in the files about Bobby wandering across the highway alone one night—"

"Oh, God."

"And something else about forgetting me at a convenience store."

"It's true," she said, pulling at her hair. "I did. I'd gone there for beer, and then I just …"

"It's okay, Mom. I'm no worse for the experience. Hell, I don't remember it at all, but I'll bet I thought it was fun at the time."

"You were hysterical," she said, "when they finally found me. If it hadn't been for Von, they'd have taken you away. But keep going. What's next?"

"We don't have to do this."

"No, I need to know. What's next?" she repeated.

"There was a report from a neighbor." I paused, but she didn't show any sign of remembering. "Apparently Bobby showed up at her house one night. Naked and … he said your friend had … that's how he said it, according to the report, 'Mommy's friend hurt—'"

"No!" she shouted. "That never … Ricky, I never *had* any—"

"I know," I said, reaching across the table to hold her hand. "It was unfounded, open and shut. According to the report, you and I were asleep in my room, and Martha was asleep in your bed. But the front door was open. Remember how Bobby used to climb everywhere? He could find his way out of anything. But there was no one else here. Aunt Von and Uncle Ben vouched for you, and so did Martha. Plus, there was no trauma to … to Bobby." She looked so confused I had to ask, "Do you remember any of this?"

"No." She shook her head. "I mean, yes, parts of it, but not *that*. I remember the cops waking us up. I remember them yelling at me about being an unfit mother. The thing was, I wasn't even drunk that night. I was stone cold sober. You and Bobby would have been about four years old at the time. I remember that, because Von and Ben had asked me to keep Martha for the night. They were on the road, going to buy some equipment for the nursery, some piece of machinery they just had to have right away, and the only place they could find it was in Miami. I don't even remember what it was now, but they knew they wouldn't be home until well after midnight, and they didn't want Martha home alone that late at night. She was always responsible, but she was still a ten-year-old girl.

"She came to spend the night, and we stayed up late, the four of us. You boys were totally wound up, what with Martha being there. Neither of you could settle down to sleep, so we decided to put in a Disney movie and pop some popcorn. We had a regular little party. You and Bobby were overjoyed by the whole thing, by the change in routine, by Martha, everything. We didn't go to bed until after midnight, and I was exhausted from the heat that day. It had been brutal out at the nursery. I took a bath, crawled in next to the two of you, and slept like a rock as soon as my head hit the pillow. Right up until the cops stormed in and woke me up.

"But I never heard *anything* about Bobby saying he'd been hurt. No one ever said that to me. They questioned Martha, and then Von and Ben, who were home by then. They looked you over, and Bobby, too. Then they left. That was it. They must have filed a report with the Department later, but I didn't know about it. One of the social workers may have visited us—I'm sure someone did—but hell, that was a regular occurrence back then.

"Ricky, there was no one here to hurt Bobby. I didn't have friends over. I'd been through so much with Vern I didn't trust myself in relationships. The last thing I wanted was another man around. When have you ever known me to even so much as go out on a date?"

She was right; my mother had never shown the least bit of interest in maintaining a relationship with anyone other than the six of us sharing that little duplex. I used to worry, after I left home, that she'd be lonely, but she was such a self-contained person she truly didn't seem to need anyone else. I guess that's what happens when you grow up without a family.

"You act as if you need to convince me," I said, "but you don't. I don't care what Gerry uncovered, except that it may hurt you. This is what will be in the paper tomorrow morning. I don't know what might happen after that. Another round of reporters, probably. Self-righteous trolls picketing in your yard. Hate mail, no doubt. I don't know, but you have to be prepared for anything. There are some crazy assholes out there. Why don't you come and stay with me for a few days? Just until all this mess blows over."

"I can't." She lay her head down and began to cry, breaking my heart in the process. "I have to be here for Bobby."

I was convinced by then that Bobby wasn't in the house. I assumed she meant, as she'd meant since the day he disappeared, she had to remain there in case he came home. "Then let me stay with you," I said. "I don't want you to face all this alone. We can both be here for Bobby, if he tries to get in touch with you."

"No." She sat up abruptly, wiping her eyes. "You're sweet, Ricky, and I appreciate it, but you've got a full plate of your own. You need to sort things out with Gerry, and Andy, too. Losing your job isn't going to help anyone. Besides, I'll be fine. I've got Von and Ben next door, and the nursery to keep me busy. I'll just avoid the news and stay off the internet, which isn't hard to do. How bad could it get, really?"

If only I had known the answer to that question in time to protect her, things might have turned out differently. But I hadn't known, nor had I known that was the last time I would see my mother.

I should have insisted she come with me. On the nights I beat myself up the most, I remind myself there's no way I could have known what was to come; I couldn't possibly have imagined things would turn out as they did. But that's small comfort, and it changes nothing.

What kind of son leaves his mother alone at a time like that?

We cleaned up the dishes, watched a Discovery channel show about crab fishermen Mom had recorded, and finally told each other good night, both of us yawning, before hugging in the doorway as I gathered my keys and wallet from the entryway table and prepared to leave. "Call me if you need anything," I said, "and I'm sorry for upsetting you. But I do want you to be prepared."

"I know, honey," she answered, touching my arm. "As much as I hated to revisit those dark times, it would be a thousand times worse to wake up to all that tomorrow without even knowing it was coming. At least now I can put up my deflector shield."

I laughed, and Mom even cracked a smile. It was an old joke from childhood, one I'd forgotten, borrowed from *Star Wars*. Bobby and I could battle for hours, but between Force cloaks and deflector shields, neither of us could ever win. "I got you," Bobby would scream, and I'd answer, "No way! You can't see me because I have a Force cloak." Or, "You're dead, Bobby," I'd yell, only to have him counter, "You didn't hit me; my deflector shield is up!" It used to drive Mom nuts, listening to us go on that way.

"But how can either of you ever win?" she'd ask. "You just keep coming up with new ways to outdo each other." She was right, but that had never seemed to bother us.

Funny, how memories of Bobby were starting to come back to me. They brought with them a sharp pang of sadness, though whether it was because I missed my brother, or because I'd forgotten him, I couldn't say.

Mom stood in the doorway, silhouetted against the lamplight, waving as I backed out of the driveway to begin the half hour trip back home. How often I've relived that moment. If I could go back in time, I'd get out of my car and take her arm, pulling her down the steps, giving her no choice but to come with me.

"No do-overs," Bobby used to say when I lost at our games, as I often did. I can still hear his little boy laughter floating on the wind, taunting me. "No do-overs! You lose!"

How right he was.

Chapter 29: Tabby

I closed the door and leaned my forehead against it, at a loss as to what to do. I had no idea what my next step should be; I only knew I needed to fix the mistakes and missteps I'd made in the past. *How* was the question to which I had no answer.

"I said *Daddy*. *Daddy's* friend, not Mommy's."

I turned to stare at Bobby. "What did you just say?"

"It was Dad's friend who molested me. Some old drunk he had living with him at that time."

"Oh, my God, Bobby." I sank to the floor, my back against the wall. "Why didn't you tell me?"

"I did," he said, "but I guess you were too drunk to remember. Some of that stuff Dad told me wasn't too far from the truth, was it?"

"What do you mean?" I struggled to look up at him, trying to ignore the spinning of the room. I didn't want to believe what he was telling me, but I had no choice.

"He said you were a drunk who couldn't take care

of us. From what I could overhear between you and Ricky tonight, sounds like Dad was right on the money, although I'd say he hardly had room to talk."

My vision faded at the edges, but I forced myself to breathe. I wouldn't allow myself to take the coward's way out; I'd remain focused and alert. This time I would hear Bobby, no matter how devastating his words might be.

"When?" I asked. "How? Bobby, help me understand."

"It doesn't matter now," he said, lowering himself to the floor across from me. "It's over and done, too late to do anything about it."

"It does matter, Bobby. I failed you, in the most unforgivable way imaginable. How can I even begin to make that up to you?"

He shrugged, picking at a worn spot on the living room carpet. "I really don't want to get into all of it, okay? It doesn't matter anymore, and there isn't much to tell. I woke up to Ricky snoring beside me and a smelly old man slobbering all over my crotch. End of story."

The thought of my baby boy waking to that horror nearly undid me. The fear he must have felt, the betrayal, realizing neither of his parents was there to protect him. Or realizing that the parent who was there didn't protect him, and the parent who wasn't there had put him in harm's way to begin with. "When?" I asked. "Where? How many times? Bobby, I have to know." I reached out for him, but he knocked my hand away.

"When I was a kid, at Dad's, and once. Does that answer everything?" He sighed. "Look. I yelled for Dad, and he and some other junkies chased the asshole out of the house and beat the hell out of him, okay? Dad told me not to tell anyone. He said if I told, the judge would make sure we never got to see each other again.

"For a while, I didn't tell, but then when it was time to go visit Dad again, I didn't want to go. I don't remember exactly what I told you. Something along the lines of Dad's friend kissing me, but you were drunk, and I knew that. I guess I thought your maternal instincts might kick in anyway and you'd help me, but you were always lacking a little in that department, weren't you?"

There are some feelings that have no words to describe them, or at least no words I know. There are probably people somewhere who know, maybe stuffy old white men who wear glasses halfway down their noses, who smoke pipes and wear tweed blazers with suede elbow patches and leather buttons, whose job it is to sit around conference tables and come up with big words to categorize and label human experiences. Those people might have been able to describe what I felt at that moment, but I couldn't.

Ricky had said I wasn't responsible for whatever Bobby had or hadn't done, but I knew better. How many chances had I blown? How many times had I failed him? I knew the answer to that. I'd had five short years to take care of him, and had failed miserably at every step. A combination of my actions and inactions shaped his world both before he was stolen, and after, too. Hell, my choices had begun to shape Bobby even before he was born, as the cocaine flowed through my system and into his. If I wasn't responsible, who was?

"I've definitely made more than my share of mistakes,"

I said, wiping at my eyes, "and there's not much doubt I was a shitty mother. I think that's obvious. But I'm hoping I can make up for some of it now. I want that more than anything in the world." Something about my response seemed to relax him. His shoulders lowered and his jaw unclenched.

"Well, at least you admit it," he said. "I guess that counts for something. Dad would never admit anything, just made excuses for himself. He couldn't see any of his own faults, but he sure as hell loved pointing out everyone else's. That's what got him killed, in the end."

Although I hadn't seen Vern in years, I knew from my own experiences there was some truth in what Bobby said. After all, his taking Bobby from me had been an attempt to make me pay for my short- comings, hadn't it? He'd been no healthier than I had, no more successful, no more stable, and yet that wasn't his focus. His focus had obviously been on me and my shortcomings. He was the arbiter of justice, so long as he didn't have to place himself in the lineup.

"Do you want a cup of tea, Bobby?" I was so drained I could barely pull myself up off the floor, but that hardly mattered. "I have decaffeinated. We can sit down and talk some more." I'd been afraid to ask what had happened between him and Vern, but I sensed he was getting ready to tell me, and I needed to know.

I believed with all my heart Vern had done something to provoke Bobby. After all, who knew more than I about the depths to which Vern could sink? I believed whatever he had done to Bobby had been something so terrible Bobby had snapped under the pressure. As much as I dreaded hearing it, I couldn't help him until I knew. I couldn't hide him forever, not in our tiny duplex, but I also wouldn't go to the authorities until I had enough information to help with his defense.

"Nah," he said. "I'm not much of a tea person." He stood, too, then pulled something from his back pocket and held it toward me. Looking closer, I could see the amber liquid sparkling in the light from the kitchen. "But I'll share this with you, if you'd like."

Whiskey, in a pint-sized bottle with a glass stopper. "Bobby, why on earth would you try to hand me something like that? After the conversation we just had? Where did you even get it?"

"Mandy," he said. "A gift to celebrate busting out of that place. She brought it when she came by this morning."

"I can't have it in my house. Surely you must know that."

"Why not?" he asked. "Afraid you'll be tempted? Maybe you're not as recovered as you think you are."

"That's possible," I said, my defenses depleted. "It owned me once; I don't want to give it the chance again, especially not now. I'm here for you, Bobby. Twenty-five years too late, maybe, but at least clean and sober this time around."

"Go to bed, Ma," he said, sounding as exhausted as I felt. "It's too late to get into any more of this shit tonight. I'm tired, and I know you are, too. Let's give it a rest."

I knew I wouldn't be able to sleep, but I also knew Bobby wanted me to leave him alone. "Is there anything you need before I go?" I asked. "Did you have a chance to eat before Ricky got here? There's plenty of food left."

"I believe I'll have some of that chicken," he said. "It was torture, hiding under your bed for hours smelling fried chicken and not able to have any."

Guilt flooded me again at the thought of him squeezed under my bed, hungry and alone while Ricky and I visited. "You could have come to join us. I'd really like Ricky to know you're here. He'd want to know, and I don't like deceiving him. Please, Bobby, let's tell him. He's missed you terribly, too, you know, and he might be able to help us. He knows people, through his job—"

Bobby snorted, pulling the stopper from his bottle with a soft *pop*. "At that piece of shit paper he works for? No thanks. You can't tell him, Ma. I can't take that chance. If you do, I'm gone, and next time I won't come back." He turned the bottle up and took a drink. "Good stuff," he said, wiping his mouth with the back of a hand. "Sure you won't have some?"

"I'm sure," I replied, "and you win, since you haven't given me any choice." I didn't think I could survive losing Bobby again. "I won't say anything to Ricky, at least not until you change your mind."

"I won't change my mind," he said, "and I'm through talking about it. I'm tired, I'm hungry, and enough shit has gone down the last few days to last me a lifetime. I told you, that's enough for tonight. Now, either share a toast with me, or point me to that chicken."

"It's in the bin in the refrigerator. Help yourself." I wasn't comfortable with either his ultimatums or his tone, but we'd have to work through those things later, when we weren't both so emotionally spent.

"Good night, Bobby-doodle," I said, standing on tiptoe to kiss him on the cheek, holding my breath against the smell of booze. For the briefest of seconds, I saw his eyes soften at my use of his old nickname. "I'll try to be quiet in the morning so I don't wake you."

Thinking of morning reminded me that Von and I hadn't even discussed morning coffee. Somehow, I knew she understood I wouldn't be there. I wondered if she'd read *Swamplands* without me, or if she'd save it so we could read it together at work, as we'd often done. It crossed my mind that I should warn her about the upcoming article, but it was much too late to call. I'd have to hope I could reach her in time in the morning.

Bobby didn't answer me, so I turned to make my way to the end of the hall, softly closing the bedroom door behind me. I stood for a moment, looking at the door, picturing the missing pieces of my heart lying scattered on the other side of it. I hadn't known it would hurt; that was the big surprise. All those years, when I dreamt of finding Bobby, I imagined the fabric of our lives stitching itself seamlessly back together, as if simply by reuniting we could overcome the rips and tears Vern's and my actions had caused. But it wasn't like that. No, instead of a seamless rejoining, it was as if the broken pieces no longer fit, and the jagged edges cut when they tried to find their way home.

I could hear Bobby moving around the kitchen on the other side of my closed door, and I put my hand on the knob, wanting to go back to him, to search his face for signs of my lost little boy. It was so hard to see the child in the hardened face of the man who'd walked in out of the rain just the day before.

But I didn't go to him, after all. Instead of turning the knob, I locked it, praying he didn't hear the soft click as the bolt slid home.

Chapter 30: Von

en, honey, please. You don't need waders today, baby. We're just going to the nursery."

"*You* might be going to the nursery, but *I'm* going fishing with Floyd," he insisted, sitting on the bed in nothing but his boxer shorts, struggling to work his bare feet into the long rubber boots without hurting his arthritic toes.

Floyd was dead, but that wasn't something I wanted to share again with Ben at six o'clock on a Saturday morning, when what I needed to be doing was cooking breakfast and getting ready to go to work. I'd told Ben at least a half-dozen times the past year that his friend was dead, gone peacefully in his sleep three years before, but he couldn't hold onto the memory, and every time I told him his grief was fresh all over again.

Before we could argue over it further, I heard Tabby's knock at the front door. Tabby has a hesitant knock, always has, as if she's afraid she might be disturbing you, even if you're expecting her. I wasn't expecting her that morning, but I thanked the Lord for intervening and answering my prayers.

"I've got to get the door, Ben," I said. "Someone's knocking." I closed our bedroom door and rushed to open the front one, pulling Tabby in so quickly I almost yanked her off her feet.

"Is it Ben?" she asked. "What can I do to help?" At that moment any hurt feelings of the previous day no longer mattered. This was my best friend, the woman who knew without me saying a word that we were off to a rough start. We'd been there before. I'd known the past couple of days couldn't last, but that didn't make Ben's slide into confusion any easier to handle.

"The best thing you could have done was to knock when you did. If you want to get some coffee started, I'll go finish taking care of Ben."

Tabby nodded, stepping into the kitchen and opening a cabinet to get the coffee filters. "Take your time," she said. "I'll get things rolling in here."

I returned to the bedroom and found Ben with one boot on, trying to fit the second one on over the first. "Baby, I have some bad news."

"What?" he asked, looking up at me. "Someone smashed the mailbox again? Goddamned vandals. I swear, Von, I'm going to kick somebody's ass—"

"No, Ben." Our mailbox hadn't been smashed in at least ten years, not since the youngest of the Hawkins clan had finally moved away. I gently pried the second boot from Ben's hands, then knelt in front of him, my hands on his bare thighs. "That was Floyd at the door. He has to cancel fishing today. He said for you to go on to the nursery with me, and he'll call you later."

"Kind of bossy, ain't he?" Ben asked. "What if I don't want to go to the nursery? And I'll tell you what, I'm getting a little tired of Floyd canceling on me." He grumbled some more, but I was relieved to see him begin to work the boot off his foot.

"Let me help you," I said, but he swatted my hands away.

"Why would I need help, woman? What I need is breakfast."

It always hurt a little when Ben's illness caused him to be short with me, but at least now he'd hopefully shower and dress without it turning into World War III. I laid out his clothes before closing the door and lingering in the hallway to offer up a silent prayer of thanks.

"All good?" Tabby asked when I joined her in the kitchen.

"I think so," I answered, inhaling the scent of frying sausage. "He was insisting he was supposed to go fishing with Floyd this morning. I didn't have it in me to hurt him all over again by telling him the truth. It was just as terrible the sixth time he learned about it as it was the first. I told him that was Floyd at the door, stopping by to cancel the fishing trip. He believed me."

Of course he'd believed me. Why wouldn't he? We'd made it through nearly forty years of marriage without a lie between the two of us, not until Ben's loosening hold on reality meant I sometimes had to alter my own reality, too. I'd learned that fighting didn't work, nor did reasoning with him and explaining why he was wrong. His world was as real to him as mine was to me. I doubt I'd handle it well, either, if someone tried to tell me what I knew to exist was just a trick of my mind. I suppose the way I handled Ben's worst moments could be considered lying, but I didn't think of it that way. I thought of it as bridging the gap between his world and mine in the most compassionate way possible.

"I'm sorry, Von." Tabby laid a hand on my arm on her way to the freezer. She'd been a rock through everything, and I appreciated her more than I knew how to say.

"I know, Tabby. Just having you here helps. But what about you? How're you doing?"

"I was just coming over to see if I could ride with you and Ben," she said, arranging frozen biscuits on a baking sheet. "I can't seem to find my keys this morning. I thought they were in my purse, but this week has been so crazy ..." She trailed off without finishing.

"That is has," I agreed. "And of course you can. You'll have to straddle the gearshift, but it isn't as if you haven't done it before. Now, why don't you hand my kitchen back over to me and step out to get the paper? You can read it to me while I cook."

"Ricky says we don't want to do that," she said. Her back was still to me as she worked over the stove, but I could have sworn I heard a catch in her voice.

"Don't want to do what? Read the paper? Why? What's happened?" I stopped rummaging through the silverware drawer, sure I'd misheard her.

"Well, you know. It's *Swamplands*." She turned to me with a shrug, and I could see the tears building up in her eyes. "It seems Gerry managed to find my old records from the Department."

"Oh, Tabby." I knew what those old records contained, of course, since I'd been with her the whole time, and I knew it wasn't good, certainly not something she'd want spread all over the internet. "Come over here, honey, and sit down." I led her to one of the barstools at the counter and nudged her onto it. I'd been so distracted by Ben I hadn't really looked at her until then, and when I did, I grew even more alarmed. She looked terrible, her face swollen and splotchy as if she'd spent the night crying.

"What is it, Tabby? There's more, isn't there?"

"There is." She nodded, tears spilling over. "But Von, I can't tell you. I want to, but I can't. Not yet. Please understand." She started to cry in earnest then, burying her face in her hands and choking on sobs. I pulled her back to her feet to give her a hug, wrapping my arms around her and rocking her back and forth, exactly the way I used to do with Martha when she was a teen and became convinced some boy- or girlfriend drama meant the end of the world.

I'd never seen Tabby so upset, not even when Bobby disappeared. Back then, she spent the first few days dulling the pain with alcohol. After that—after treatment—she was shell-shocked for years. Sometimes I thought she still was.

This time, whatever pain had hold of her was raw and exposed, and I was afraid of the pure strength of it. She leaned into me, her whole body shaking with the crying, and I could feel the tears slipping through her fingers and soaking the front of my blouse. I didn't know what to say to her, so I hummed instead, nothing in particular, just something that came from within me, something to let her know I was there.

We stayed that way until the sausage started to burn and Ben came stomping through, still buckling his belt. "What's got into you, Von? Smells like burning—" He stopped, taking in the sight before him, me holding tight to Tabby and her squalling like a banshee. "What the hell?"

"She lost her keys," was all I could think to say as I stroked Tabby's back and let her cry it out.

"Well, damn, Tabby," he said. "It's not worth all that, is it? We have extras, remember? We can get some new ones made."

We stood there for several more minutes while Ben flipped over sausage patties, shaking his head and grunting, seemingly perplexed by the foolishness of it all.

Chapter 31: Ricky

As if I weren't in enough trouble with Andy, I had to call him five minutes after I was already late to tell him I might not make it to work at all.

"What the fuck, Ricky? You need to get your act together."

"I know," I said, "and I'm trying, but someone robbed me."

"Did you say robbed? Where are you? I'll get Gerry right on it. Who have you told? I want us to be the first ones there."

"Okay, 'robbed' was probably the wrong word. Stolen is more accurate. There's no need to send Gerry. I'm stranded at the Circle K on Lake Mary Boulevard. I'm flat on empty, so I stopped to get gas only to find out everything in my wallet has been stolen. Credit cards, debit card, license, everything. Even my Starbucks card, and you know how I need my coffee." I was trying to inject a little humor to pave the way with Andy, but he never was one for humor, not even *good* humor, which mine admittedly wasn't.

He grunted, and I could almost feel him losing interest. If I didn't have a story to deliver, he had no interest in wasting time talking to me. "What do you want me to do about it?" he finally asked.

"Nothing. I mean, nothing other than cut me a little slack. I already called a friend to come and get me, but I'm going to have to go by the bank, which closes at one. I also have to call and cancel my credit cards. I guess I should go by the police station, but I don't think there's much they can do about it since I have no idea when it happened. I don't think I've opened my wallet since Thursday, when we stopped to get gas on the way out of Tampa. The DMV will have to wait until Monday, and I'll have to either bribe the Circle K manager not to have my car towed, or bribe a friend to put gas in it and drive it to my apartment. I don't have any cash, and I can't drive without a license." I was thinking out loud, more than anything. Andy didn't care about either my problems or my plan of action, other than how either might impact him and the paper.

"So to cut through all the bullshit," he said, as if to prove my point, "what you're telling me is I've got to call Gerry in on his day off to cover for you."

"I'm sorry, Andy, but there isn't much I can do about it."

"You can come in tomorrow," he said.

"On Sunday? Are you serious? I have vacation time." Gerry and I ordinarily had a rotating sort of schedule to ensure we both got a couple of days off per week. His current days off were Friday and Saturday, and mine were Sunday and Monday. We also had half a dozen journalism interns from the university to cover for us not only when we needed time off, but also when we were out of the office covering a story. There was no need for Gerry to have to go in for me, nor was there a need for me to have to make it up to him on Sunday. Andy was just being Andy, which was to say, *difficult.*

"Damn right I'm serious. I'm not going to keep Gerry here all day on a Saturday so you can go out gallivanting around."

"Can't you call in one of the interns? They need the hours, anyway."

"There's too much going on to hand it over to some greenhorn who doesn't know the difference between a roundup and a shirttail. Your paid time off request is denied. Have your ass in here by seven to-morrow morning." He slammed down the phone.

I stood for a moment in the foggy, early morning parking lot of Circle K, grateful to have at least been able to drive my car away from the gas pump to park it by the convenience store before it ran completely out of fumes. I knew what I had to do. I'd go to the office on Sunday, as Andy had ordered, partly because it wouldn't be fair to Gerry not to. He deserved a day off, even if he was an ass. That was the other reason I'd go in: I didn't want to piss Gerry off more than I already had. I couldn't imagine any information out there he hadn't already managed to uncover, but I didn't want to do anything to spur him on to look harder.

So I'd go in Sunday and do a bang-up job, leaving everything in perfect order for Monday morning. As perfect as is possible, anyway, in a career that de-mands twenty-four hours of clickbait headlines and an endless scramble for subscribers. And then I'd quit. Hell, I remember thinking, I might even have a little fun with it, maybe write an announcement to stick somewhere back in the pages of *Swamplands*, something clickbait worthy like, *Disgruntled Journalist Considers Going Postal, Opts to Quit Instead.*

I had enough savings to last a little while—one of the benefits of being a single, childless thirty-year-old man—and if that ran out before I could find something, I knew my mother would always let me come home. It would suck, moving back in with my mother, not because of anything she'd do, but because I'd feel like a loser. Weighing all sides, though, I realized I'd rather feel like a loser than a sellout, especially when what I'd been selling was my soul.

Such were my plans as I pressed the key fob to lock my car with a wimpy-sounding *beep*, then walked to my friend's car, mentally preparing for the ribbing he would no doubt deliver. That's not at all the way it turned out, of course, because I hadn't been the only one making plans. But I hadn't known that at the time.

Chapter 32: Von

The upheaval of the morning didn't seem to want to let up anytime soon. I found the extra set of keys Tabby had given Ben and me, but she was in such terrible shape I couldn't let her drive. I tried to make her take the day off, but she wasn't having it. "Saturday is the busiest day," she said. "You're going to have your hands full, especially with …" She glanced over at Ben, who was finishing up his coffee. "I'll have plenty of time Sunday and Monday to worry about everything. I won't bail on you today."

We finally made it to the nursery, Tabby with swollen eyes and a bad case of the hiccups, me with a stained and wrinkled blouse, and Ben lamenting the fact his fishing trip had been cancelled again and he was saddled with a couple of crazy women. Thank goodness we could count on Ted to keep things running in an organized manner. He'd already unlocked the gate and opened up the office by the time we arrived to find him with a shovel and a wheelbarrow of crushed shells, filling in the potholes the rain of a couple of days before had left in our parking area.

"Morning, folks," he said by way of greeting. "I meant to get these filled in yesterday, but couldn't quite get to it." He couldn't get to it because Tabby had been so late, but he was considerate enough not to point that out. "Figured all the traffic we get in here on Saturday mornings would tear the parking lot all to hell if I didn't get an early start. Just about got it done, though, and right on time." He nodded toward the highway, where a couple of trucks were lined up, blinkers on, to turn into our place.

The entire day passed like that, family after family turning in to load up on mulch, sod, rocks, and enough plants to line I-4 with flowers and vegetables from Daytona to Orlando. Beautiful spring weather brings something out in people, makes them want to dig in the earth and get their hands dirty. We all—the four of us—knew most of the plants would be dead by August, the flower-planting moms of May tired of watering and pruning in the summer heat. Weeds would grow through the rocks, mulch would wash away in afternoon thunderstorms, and kids would realize that the idea of a vegetable garden was a lot more fun than the reality of one.

The families, not knowing what we knew, were excited. They mixed and matched flowers and debated the pros and cons of termite-treated mulch while kids ran wild, running through the rows and knocking over plants. Tabby, who has more patience than I do, followed along behind people picking up trash, collecting discarded plants, and righting upturned pots.

"Are these Vidalia?" one woman asked Ben, holding up a bag of bulbs.

"Are we in Georgia?" was Ben's answer, a smart-alecky retort he'd never have given if he'd been thinking straight. I intervened before he could do any further damage.

"Technically the Vidalia is a Georgia onion," I said with a laugh meant to lighten the mood. "Ours are St. Augustine Sweets, just as good, but local." I placed a netted bag in her hands before she could escape.

It was a blessing, really, that we were so busy. In spite of a couple of awkward moments, Ben had a decent day. He was in his element talking plants. It hardly mattered if his mind was caught in 1984, 2011, or 2014, tomatoes with end rot still needed more calcium in the soil, and crepe myrtles still needed at least eight hours of sun. Tabby didn't have time to dwell on her troubles, and I didn't have time to worry about Tabby.

We ate lunch on the run and finally had to lock the gate against newcomers at 6:15, forty-five minutes past closing time. Ben was napping back in one of the old bedrooms, and we decided to leave him be while we took inventory and cashed out the register. Ted left to drop money off in the night deposit at the bank, which left Tabby and me alone since the first time that morning.

"How are you holding up?" I asked, propping my tired feet on the desk and leaning back in my chair.

Tabby was sitting across from me, not so much slouched in her chair as sunken into it. She didn't answer me right away, apparently taking a minute to assess her state of mind. "I wish I could say I'm okay, Von, but the truth is, I'm not. This whole thing with Bobby has brought back a lot of painful memories."

It was on the tip of my tongue to ask if she'd heard from him, but once again, I decided it was better not to know. Instead of putting Tabby in a position to have to lie to me, or me in a position to have to call the cops on her, I ignored the obvious questions and settled on, "I know, honey. It was a terrible time."

I wish now I hadn't settled. Everything might have turned out differently if I'd asked the questions I wanted to ask. At the time I'd thought I was somehow protecting Tabby, but as it turned out, remaining silent was the absolute worst thing I could have done. I can't forgive myself for that.

"I don't just mean his disappearance," she was saying, "I mean me, how I was. I look back, and for the life of me I don't understand how I could have been so careless with them." She spoke so quietly I could hardly hear her.

"Tabby, I think you're being a little too hard on yourself," I said. "Did you make mistakes? Sure. But you also loved your children. No one ever doubted that. You couldn't have kept Vern from taking Bobby. If he hadn't gotten him then, he'd have come back for a second try and for all we know, taken both of them."

"I appreciate what you're trying to do," she said, "and who knows? Maybe you're right. Maybe Vern would have just kept coming until he got what he wanted, but you can't argue the fact that I made it easy for him. I can't even pinpoint exactly when I started to screw everything up. I've tried. I spent all night last night trying. You'd think as someone who'd spent her whole childhood wanting a momma, I'd have worked harder at being one, wouldn't you?"

"This is what I mean about you being too hard on yourself," I said. "You broke the cycle. Your mother was abused and she abused you, but you never abused your children, not even at the worst of times. Look at how Ricky turned out. He's a fine man. How do you think he got that way if not for you?"

"I think it's just him," she said with a shrug. "Something special in him that made him turn out okay in spite of me. I didn't abuse them if you mean hitting, beating, that sort of thing. Things that were done to me. But how many times was I too drunk to know where they were or what they were doing? Or what was being done to them?" The tears welled up again and she let them fall. "Do you remember the time Martha spent the night with us and Bobby took off after we all fell asleep?"

"I do, but you hadn't been drinking that night. You were exhausted. It was unfair of Ben and me to have asked you to keep Martha."

She shook her head, dismissing my attempt at an apology. "Just listen, okay? That night was in the records Gerry found for his *Swamplands* article. Ricky warned me about it. Do you know what Bobby told the neighbor who found him?"

I thought back to that night. Ben and I had arrived home after midnight to a scene no mother wants to see: a yard full of patrol cars and an ambulance parked on the street. "What I remember most is the way my heart dropped when I saw all the flashing lights, then the absolute relief when I counted three kids, all very much alive, bouncing on your couch while a deputy read you the riot act. When we found out what had happened I remember thinking, 'Well, of course it was Bobby.' But I don't remember anything specific he said."

"He said someone had touched him. Inappropriately."

"*What?* Who?" My feet came off the desk with a *bang*, and I sat up so quickly my chair nearly rolled out from under me.

She hesitated. "He didn't say who, exactly, and apparently they didn't find enough evidence to even warrant investigating. I've tried to think back, to remember if he acted any differently or if there were any signs, but I probably wouldn't have been sober enough to know."

"Your memory is playing tricks on you, Tabby," I said. "It wasn't as if you were drunk all the time. You would go days without drinking. We had good times, a lot of them. We practically lived on the beach with those kids; remember how brown they'd get? They used to compare their skin to Martha's." I laughed at the memory. I hadn't thought of that in years.

"You took them to scouts and to story hour at the library," I reminded her, "and signed them up for t-ball and tumbling classes at the YMCA. It's true that when you started drinking you kept at it until you passed out, but that wasn't an everyday thing. There were some bad days, I won't lie, some downright *terrible* days, but there were many more good days than bad."

I looked over at her, but she refused to look back at me. "Now, maybe someone touched Bobby, or maybe the neighbor misunderstood what he said. Or maybe … well, I won't even say that out loud." Maybe he was lying, I wanted to say, since Bobby had sometimes played fast and loose with the truth. But Tabby had always been defensive when it came to

Bobby, and I didn't want a rehash of one of our old arguments decades after the fact. "I doubt we'll ever know what really happened," I said instead, "but you won't get anywhere beating yourself over the head with something written in a casefile twenty-five years ago. What good could that possibly do?"

She sat quietly for so long I reached for my purse, about to suggest we head home, before she spoke. "Why do you think Bobby did it, Von? Why do you think he killed Vern?"

I sat back again, studying her face. "I suppose the easy answer would be that he did it in self-defense," I said. "Or maybe to pay Vern back for whatever wrongs he felt were done to him."

"What's the hard answer?" she asked.

"Just about anything else," I said. "I imagine we'd all like to think Bobby wouldn't have hurt Vern if Vern didn't somehow deserve it, but we don't really know that, do we? And no matter how you look at it, it's impossible to justify what he did to those two guards."

"What if there's something wrong with him?" she asked. "What if by the time I stopped using, it was already too late? Remember how he used to scream? Or what if he felt abandoned by me, not just when Vern took him, but before, when I was drunk or passed out? Ricky said Gerry found an expert to interview, someone who talked about all the bad things that can happen when parents don't bond right with their kids. What if he's right?"

"Is that what this is about?" I asked, a little spark of anger flaring somewhere behind my eyes. "You trying to find a way to take the blame for Bobby? Don't you dare do it," I said, raising my voice. "I watched you make excuses for that child from the time he was born until the day he disappeared. Don't do it, Tabby. That isn't fair to you or to Bobby, and it sure as hell isn't fair to Ricky."

"I'm just trying to understand, Von. I need to know if Bobby did the things he did because of something *I* did first. I don't think babies are born bad; I think something happens to them to make them that way. What if I'm what happened to Bobby?"

I was so irritated with Tabby at that moment I wanted to shake her. "First of all," I said, counting off on my fingers, "he's been gone from you for way longer than you had him. If someone shaped him to be bad, it wasn't you. Second, he's a grown man capable of making choices. Regardless of whether or not he thinks they deserved it—which, by the way, isn't his call to make—he made a choice that had nothing to do with you. And third"—I stood, grabbing my purse from under the desk—"I do believe sometimes babies are just born bad."

I moved toward the hallway, going to wake Ben and praying he'd be in a good mood when I did. "Now let's get out of here," I said to Tabby over my shoulder. "This day has lasted too long, already."

None of us said much on the drive home. Maybe we were all too tired. Or maybe Ben was lost in time, Tabby was lost in her head, and I was just too damn irritated.

Chapter 33: Tabby

I helped Von get Ben inside and settled before hugging her and leaving for my own place. Just as I fitted my borrowed key into the lock, she stuck her head back out of her door and called to me. "What are you doing Monday night, Tabby?"

I smiled, because I knew why she was asking. "I don't have any plans," I said. "Did you have something in mind?"

"I think it's time for a tune-up," she said, "time to work the program, so be ready at six-thirty sharp." She closed the door and I laughed for the first time in days. A "tune-up" was our way of saying we needed to go back to the support meeting at the church. They still met a couple of times a week, but Von and I no longer went regularly. We were so far into sobriety by then I don't think either of us ever seriously considered backsliding. Still, it was nice to go every so often, to be among people who recognized parts of us no one else could and still never passed judgement.

I most definitely needed a tune-up, I was thinking to myself as I stepped inside and found the place completely dark. I always left a light on for myself, but I'd either forgotten that morning, or Bobby had turned it off. I flipped on the living room light, closing the door behind me before calling softly for Bobby. "It's just me, honey. Are you here?"

No answer. I glanced around to see everything in order, with the exception of a pile of dirty dishes in the kitchen sink. "Bobby?" I called again, starting down the hallway, looking into the open rooms. Everything was exactly as it should have been, complete with set of keys on top of my dresser, on the side closest to the bedroom door. I must have set them down at some point during my hectic morning, and then forgotten about them. At least I could get Von's keys back to her in the morning.

I did one more quick check of the house. Bobby was definitely gone, but it looked as if he planned on coming back, at least temporarily. There was a stack of folded clothes on his bed, shirts and jeans I recognized as the ones Ricky kept at the house, and next to that, a suitcase that had been stored in the top of my closet. Curious, I stepped closer. Partially hidden by the suitcase was a Rand McNally Road Atlas from 2002. Ricky had used it in his high school geography class during senior year.

Inside the suitcase was my lockbox, the one that until recently had contained my .38. I reached for the lock, turning the numbers into place. It remained locked. I stood back, letting it sink in. Bobby had changed the combination.

But why?

I didn't have time to ponder that question before all hell broke out. First, Ricky called. I grabbed my phone on the way out to the porch. I needed the cooler night air to clear my thoughts. As I closed the door behind me, a lone deputy drove by, maybe just making his rounds, maybe, as I suspected, keeping an eye out for Bobby. At least the reporters were gone.

"Hey, Mom," Ricky greeted me. "I just wanted to check in to see how you're doing."

"Busy day," I said. "You know how Saturdays are. How are you?"

"*Pffftt*," he responded, a sound of irritation. "Someone took all the stuff out of my wallet."

"What?"

"Yeah. Driver's license, the works. I don't guess there's any chance you've seen any of it around there?"

"No, honey, I'd have called right away."

"I know you would have, but I had to ask. I cancelled everything today, but I can't get to the DMV until Monday, so I'm stuck here until then."

"Oh, honey." I sank into a porch chair. "I'm so sorry. Is there anything I can do?"

"Nope," he said. "Just wanted to let you know I can't get there this weekend. On top of everything else, Andy's making me work tomorrow. I have to be there at seven. I'm staying with Greg tonight because he's giving me a ride, and he lives a lot closer to the office than I do."

Greg was an old friend of Ricky's from high school. I was glad they'd remained close through the years, and relieved Greg was there to help Ricky out when he needed it.

"Tell Greg hello for me, and thank him for me, too," I said.

"I will," Ricky promised. "Are you sure everything's okay there?"

"We're all good here, honey, but keep me posted, okay? Let me know how things go at the DMV Monday."

"I'll let you know in person as soon as I have a license again," he said. "I'm going to turn in my resignation tomorrow."

"Ricky, are you sure about this?" I'd known Ricky would eventually leave *Swamplands* behind, but I hadn't expected it at that particular moment.

"Very sure. I've wanted out of there for a long time. I kept telling myself *Swamplands* was a stepping stone, but it's more like quicksand."

"I have to admit, I'll be happy to see you get out of there. You're too good for that place, honey. I don't think I knew just how bad it was until Gerry bribed his way into my old records. You can do much better than that."

He laughed. "Well, you might be a little biased."

I smiled. "Not a chance. You're welcome to move back home, you know." As I said it, a jolt of panic shot through me. *But what about Bobby?*

"Thanks, but I don't think it'll come to that," Ricky said, and I breathed a sigh of relief. "I've got plenty of savings. I'll find something soon. It might not be something in journalism, at least not right away, but anything is better than continuing to work for Andy."

"Give me a call tomorrow and let me know how it goes, will you? I don't imagine Andy handling things very well. I guess we're lucky all the dirt on us has already been dug. There isn't much else he can do."

"True, that," he said. "I'll call you tomorrow evening just so you'll know I made it out alive."

I laughed, not yet aware of how dangerously close to the truth his words were.

I'd no sooner hung up my phone than Von came bursting out of their door, her phone in hand. "Tabby, it's Martha. She's on her way here, about twenty minutes out. She says there's something we need to know. Hold on." She went back to conversing with Martha as I stood and waited, mosquitos nipping at my ankles.

"She's bringing a pastor with her," said Von. "Vern's pastor."

"Vern had a pastor?" I hadn't meant to speak the question aloud, but it had burst out, anyway.

Von held up a finger, shushing me, but I couldn't have said anything else, anyway, since just then my own phone rang again with a call from Ted. I could count on one hand the number of times Ted had called me, all when Ben and Von had been out of town. I had a bad feeling as I clicked to answer.

"Tabby? I've been trying to reach Von but she isn't answering."

"She's on the other line with Martha. What's up? Is everything okay?"

"I'm afraid it isn't," he said. "I'm at the hospital."

"*What?*" My screech caught Von's attention, and it was my turn to hold up a finger to shush her. "What on earth, Ted?" I put my phone on speaker so Von could listen in.

"Got jumped at the night deposit," he said. "Some guy wearing a ski cap. Whacked my arm with a damned crowbar and ran off with the bag when I dropped it."

"Are you okay?"

"They seem to think my arm is broken," he said, "but I'll be all right. I feel terrible about the money, though."

Von had ended her call with Martha by that time, and she grabbed my phone out of my hand. "I don't care about the money, Ted, I care about you," she yelled at the phone. "Are you at Memorial? I'll be right there."

"No need, Von. Sarah's here, and you know how she is. She'll drive me crazy enough with her nursing; I don't need you here, too. I gotta run. Cops are here with more questions for me. I'll have to give them your information, too. I don't know if they'll be by your place tonight or tomorrow, but they'll need to confirm things with you. Amount of the deposit, time I left the nursery, that kind of thing."

"We'll be here whenever they show up," said Von. "I'm so sorry about this, Ted. I should have come with you. Tabby could have stayed with Ben. We'll file a workers' comp claim and Ben and I will take care of anything it doesn't cover. Don't you and Sarah worry about that."

Von's policy had always been to send two with the deposit, but that had gone by the wayside when Ben became ill. More often than not, Ted volunteered to go alone, and since we were often a hand short at the nursery, Von had let him.

"Don't even start thinking that way, Von," said Ted. "No one could have seen this coming, and I don't want you and Ben sitting there feeling guilty. I just hope they get the bastard and recover your money."

"Ted McGillis," Von warned through tears, "if you mention money one more time, I swear I'll come down there and break your other arm. I just need you to be okay."

"Careful with those threats, Von." Ted chuckled on the other end. "I'm surrounded by cops. They might hear you. Now, I really do have to go. As patient as these uniforms are being, I think they're getting a little tired of waiting for me."

"Have Sarah call me with updates," said Von. "I want to know everything."

"I'll tell her," he said, "but be careful what you wish for. You know how my wife is; she'll be calling you every ten minutes."

Ted ended the call and Von and I stood there, staring at each other. "The world has gone crazy this week," she finally said, just before Martha's headlights washed over us as she pulled into the driveway.

Chapter 34: Tabby

We gathered in Von's living room, Von, Ben, Martha, Reverend Hayes, and me. Von, ever the proper hostess, offered to make coffee—"It's decaf," she assured us—but everyone declined. As we took our seats, no one seemed to know where to start.

"You were Vern's minister?" I finally asked, still having a hard time wrapping my head around that one.

"I was," Reverend Hayes confirmed. He was a heavy man, balding and pink-skinned, and his cheeks jiggled when he nodded. "Vern had been a part of our congregation for about the last six months. I first met him at one of the support meetings held in the church basement. I invited him to church, of course, just like I invite everyone to our church. I have to admit I was surprised he took me up on it. Most people don't. I'm afraid our little congregation is dying out." The light reflecting off his glasses kept me from seeing his eyes, but I would have bet money he was close to tears with that admission.

"Vern was attending support meetings?" I was even more surprised at that news.

"He was. I don't know how long he'd been attending, but I never knew him as anything but clean and sober, if a little slow."

A clean and sober Vern was hard to imagine. I'd never seen him that way, not even when we first met. No doubt he *was* slow, after all the poison he'd put into his body over the years. Before I could continue with my line of questioning, Von spoke up.

"Martha said you had something to share with us," she prompted. "What is it?"

Reverend Hayes sighed. "I'm afraid it's going to be quite upsetting," he said. "I've been working closely with the police in Tampa, and there are things I think you deserve to know. I managed to track down Martha through her friend at the police department. I was concerned, you see, because you can't adequately protect yourself if you don't know the truth."

Von and I exchanged a look. "What truth is that?" she asked.

The reverend shifted in his seat. "Vern had come to me for guidance," he said. "He had come across some very disturbing information regarding Bobby. He knew what he needed to do, but was having a hard time reconciling his head with his heart."

"Go on," I said. He seemed to be taking an exceptionally long time telling us whatever it was he thought we needed to know.

He cleared his throat, and Von jumped up to fetch him a glass of water. "Thank you," he said, taking a sip and dabbing at his forehead with a handkerchief. "I'm afraid none of this is going to be easy to hear."

"Reverend," said Ben, the first time he'd spoken. "Just skip over all the warnings and get to it. At the rate you're going, I'll be dead of old age before I ever learn what it is you're trying to say."

Martha shot her dad a disapproving look, but his rebuke seemed to do the trick. Reverend Hayes sat up straighter. "Have you heard of the Silk Stocking Rapist?"

Whatever I'd been expecting him to say, that wasn't it. Of course we'd heard of him. It had been all over the news several months before. *Swamplands* had had articles on it for days on end. Four women raped, three of them murdered. One of them had survived and the media, *Swamplands* in particular, had had a field day sifting through the details of her past, speculating on why she'd been chosen by the rapist. None of us seemed able to speak, so we nodded instead.

"The police have reason to believe it's Bobby, based on what Vern said he'd found."

"Vern was a drug-addled, kidnapping, abusive asshole," I said, rising from my chair. "He'd say or do anything to hurt anyone who went against him. How could you even suggest—"

"Tabby." Von grabbed my arm, turning me to face her. "Sit down and listen. Right now."

I sat, still unable to stomach what this sweaty man of God was saying, but without the energy to go against Von.

"I'm sorry." Von was apologizing for me. "You can imagine how difficult all this is. She's not herself. Now, what makes the police think Bobby is the one committing the crimes?" Von kept her hand tight on my arm.

"Vern found a box of keepsakes," the reverend replied. "Bobby was still living with him. As far as I know, he'd never lived anywhere else. It was … it wasn't the cleanest home. They had a pretty bad bug infestation. Cockroaches. It had gotten so bad they were being bitten as they slept. I guess that was what finally prompted Vern to call an exterminator. In the process of taking the exterminator through the place to set out bait, Vern came across a cardboard box in Bobby's closet. For whatever reason, that specific box seemed even more infested than the surrounding items."

"I don't think I can listen to this," I said, turning to Von.

"You can," she said. "You have to. Keep going," she said, turning back to Reverend Hayes. "What was in the box?"

"Pinky fingers," he said, "at least according to Vern."

At first I thought I must have misheard him, but his next words left no doubt as to what he'd said. "The authorities haven't released that detail to the media. The Silk Stocking Rapist removes the tip of each victim's right pinky finger."

"Good God," Von breathed beside me.

"Told you that boy wasn't no angel," said Ben, from somewhere over to my left.

"Go ahead and finish it for them, Reverend," said Martha. "I don't think they can take much more."

"Vern called me after that to set up an appointment. He was a wreck when I met with him that afternoon. He told me the whole story, how he'd kidnapped Bobby, how he'd wanted both boys but could only get to one. He said he'd never have done it except Bobby had started talking, telling people about an incident in his father's house. Did you know about that?"

"Only recently," I managed to say, ignoring Von's look.

"Vern was afraid he'd lose contact with the boys if word got out about the molestation. He was convinced you'd take him to court," he looked at me, "and he'd lose parental rights. He wasn't thinking too clearly at the time, he freely admitted that, and his solution was to take them and run. From what I gather, they lived a pretty hard life. You can imagine."

I could, and I had, for years.

"He was sorry," the reverend continued. "He'd gotten sober, and finally had to face what he'd done. He was actively working his program, and he knew he needed to make amends. He was working on how to do that when he found the box."

"What did he do with it?" Von asked. I'd wondered, too, but I couldn't catch my breath long enough to ask.

"First, he came to me and confessed what he'd found. Neither of us knew its significance at that time, but a box of fingers … well, it obviously wasn't anything good. You have to understand, Vern had enormous guilt. He was insightful enough to know his actions had hurt Bobby. He blamed himself for any trouble his son got into, and because of that, he was reluctant to contact the police. We prayed together, and Vern came to understand he'd be hurting not only past and future victims by keeping the box a secret, but also Bobby. Bobby needed help, and he couldn't get it if Vern kept his secret."

"So he decided to turn Bobby in," said Von.

"He did," the reverend confirmed, "but he was killed before he could."

"You think Bobby found out what Vern planned to do, so he shot him," said Martha.

"I'd almost guarantee it," said Reverend Hayes. "The Silk Stocking Rapist is a very sick individual. A sociopath who's only interested in meeting his own needs, and God help—I mean this literally—anyone who gets in his way."

"What happened to the box?" Von asked. "Do the police have it now?"

The reverend shook his head, his cheeks following along a quarter-second behind. "I went to the police as soon as I learned about Vern's murder," he said. "I told them what Vern had shared with me, but as of yet, the box hasn't been found."

"Aunt Tabby," Martha spoke my name gently. "Do you know where Bobby is?"

I don't know if I would have answered had we not been interrupted by a knock on the door. It was the sheriff's department, coming to talk to Von about Ted. Martha jumped up to help get her father ready for bed, while Von waved the deputies in and the reverend stood against the wall looking awkward and out of place.

I chose that moment to leave, but not before Ben saw me.

"You think on things," he called to me as I slipped out the door. "Make the right decision, Tabby. I have faith in you. We all do."

I hurried back to my place without answering him, letting myself in and locking the door behind me. There was something I had to know. I yanked the junk drawer in the kitchen open hard enough to leave it hanging off its track. Grabbing a hammer and a screwdriver, I headed toward Bobby's bedroom before I could lose my nerve.

It took five tries before I could pop the lock on my old lockbox. No fingers, thank God, but what it did contain was in some ways worse. I wish I could say I was surprised, but after all I'd just heard, I was not. I sat on my sons' old bedroom floor, surrounded by the model rockets and solar systems I'd refused to let Ricky take down, and picked each item up, one by one. Ricky's birth certificate, taken from the fireproof file cabinet in my closet. Ricky's driver's license and credit cards. Von's house and truck keys. My .38.

Even I, with all my protective momma-bear instincts, had to acknowledge the truth at that point. After all, I wasn't momma bear to just one, but to two. Bobby must have waited until we were either caught up in our T.V. show or nodding off before he crept out to take the contents of Ricky's wallet. And I hadn't lost my keys; Bobby had taken them and somehow made copies—my bet was on the Hawkins girl—including the extra sets I had for Von and Ricky. As for the .38, he'd clearly watched me stow the gun under my car seat, peeking, I assumed, between the closed blinds as I prepared to leave.

He had his identical twin's clothes, identification, and keys. He also had a gun. I didn't know where Bobby was at that moment, but I sent up a prayer of thanks Ricky wasn't home. How ironic that Bobby's theft of Ricky's license meant Ricky wouldn't be home if Bobby showed up to do harm. It was a crazy plan he'd come up with, but not an impossible one. If

Bobby kept his nose clean, if he stayed out of trouble and away from fingerprinting, it might just work.

I could have gone back to Von's place and gotten the deputies. I could have confessed I'd known where Bobby was all along. I could have done either of those things, but I didn't. I had some amends of my own I needed to make.

What I did do was pick up the .38 from the pile at my feet, click it open again, and check the bullets, just to be safe. I gathered the other contents back into the lockbox and stood, holding it in my left hand while tucking the gun into my waistband with my right. I went into the kitchen, placed the busted lockbox with its contents in the middle of the kitchen table, and took a seat.

Then I waited.

Chapter 35: Tabby

The sun is just coming over the horizon, turning the dark of my kitchen into a soft gray, when I hear Bobby's new key in the back door. I've left the storm door unlatched for him. He doesn't see me at first, focused as he is on scanning the backyard and the undeveloped land behind us. The deputies are long gone from Von's place by now, and I wonder if Bobby even knows they were there. Probably so, I think, because Bobby seems to have a way of knowing everything.

He's carrying something in his right hand, but I can't quite make out what it is. Apparently satisfied he's made it home undetected, he closes both doors, locking them, before turning to see me at the table.

"Holy shit, you scared me," he says, walking toward me. He stops halfway to the table, his eyes finding the busted box in its center. For a split second he looks caught, like he used to look when I found him stealing cookies from the pantry, but he quickly masks it, a cold smile spreading across his features instead.

"You found it," he says. "I'd have bet anything you wouldn't go snooping through my things."

"It's never safe to make a bet like that," I say. "I've lost my fair share of them in the last few hours."

He raises his eyebrows and pulls out the chair across from me, dropping a Von's Plants and Such moneybag on the table next to the box. I do my best to hide my reaction. Of course it was him; I should have known. "Do tell," he says. "What bets have you lost?"

"For starters, the one in which I said you were innocent," I say, "and the one in which I said you'd never hurt your brother. I'm sure there are others."

"You hadn't bet against me hurting you?"

"I hadn't bet on that one," I say, "but only because I don't particularly care if you do."

"I see," he says, leaning back in the chair. "A pity party for Mom, who's been so mistreated and misunderstood she no longer cares whether she lives or dies."

I don't answer him. I just sit waiting to see what he'll do next.

"Where's the gun?" he asks after a moment. "Back in the car?"

"Wouldn't have done much good for me to put it back there, would it?"

"Doesn't matter," he says with a shrug. "If I planned to kill you, I wouldn't need a gun to do it."

"Do you?" I ask. "Plan to kill me, I mean."

He leans close, staring into my face in the dim light. I can just make out the brown speck in the middle of all the blue of his right eye. I have loved this child, that brown speck, those blue eyes. For years, I dreamt of those eyes, bargaining with both God and

Satan, promising my very soul if one of them would bring my child back to me.

One of them did.

"I think it might be more cruel to let you live," he says, before sitting back again. "It'll make it harder for me, of course, but nothing's ever easy. I assume you've warned Ricky? He wasn't home when I stopped by earlier."

My veins turn to ice, but I only shake my head. "No," I say. "I haven't, and there's no need to now."

"I suppose you're right," he agrees, misunderstanding me. "You've ruined that plan, haven't you? I'll just have to come up with another one." He stands, unzipping the moneybag and shoving Ricky's items inside. "Luckily for me, you guys had a busy day at the nursery. This'll give me a good start." He lifts his shirt—Ricky's shirt, the faded Miami Dolphins t-shirt he wears when helping me with jobs around the house—and sucks in his stomach, pushing the bag down into fashionably ripped jeans he no doubt found in Ricky's apartment.

I know he still plans to kill Ricky. Maybe not today. Maybe not this year. But he will, eventually. Why else would he still need Ricky's identification? It's a built-in escape route provided by a quirk of nature thirty years ago in my womb. It's also the perfect way to destroy me, which seems to be something Bobby wants to do.

"Did you rape those women, Bobby?" I ask. I don't really expect an answer, but he surprises me.

"The four they know of, you mean? I did. A couple of others, too, but I suppose no one cares enough to wonder where they went."

"That's why you killed Vern," I say, "because he was about to figure it out."

"Because he was about to turn me in," he says, "which isn't quite the same thing. Do you know how many times I could have turned him in but didn't? For running off with me, for letting his friend grope all over me, for shooting up and toking up and all-around fucking up? But *he* was going to turn *me* in. Can you believe that?"

There's no regret in his voice as he speaks to me. There's nothing but anger and self-pity.

"And now you plan to just walk out of here and disappear?" I ask. "I can't let you do that."

"You won't stop me," he says, grabbing my chin and yanking me to face him. Something pops deep in my neck. Pain shoots down my arm, but I don't care. I can feel his breath, hot against my face. "I'm your Bobby-doodle, remember? You'd do anything for me. You have to, because you're the one who made me the way I am. That tortures you, doesn't it? Keeps you awake at night?" He lets go of my chin and steps back. "I'll let you live so you can torture yourself, and you'll let me go because you have to. I'd bet my life on it."

He smiles his crooked smile one last time before he turns and walks to the door, surveying the yard again before unlatching the storm door and stepping outside. He walks toward the trees. It's lighter now. He'll have to walk quickly to avoid being seen, but that's okay. I'm ready.

I go and stand in the open door, watching him. I let him get about twenty feet away before I call his name. "Bobby."

He hesitates, but doesn't look back. That's the way

we'll do it, then.

I never was any good at working through step nine, the one about making amends. Partly, that's because I hadn't known where Bobby was in order to make amends. Partly, it's because I was so caught up in missing Bobby I knowingly hurt Ricky in hundreds of little ways throughout his life. And finally, maybe most importantly, it's because it's impossible to know how to make amends for having given birth to an evil child.

I'm not as clueless as Von and Ben think I am. I know my children. I don't know if I caused Bobby to be the way he is, or if, like Von said, he was just born that way. In the end it doesn't matter because the solution is the same, either way.

You make sure Ricky comes first this time, Von had said.

I will, Von.

It's time to complete the ninth step. I'm sure this isn't the decision Ben meant for me to make when he advised me to make the right one, but it *is* the right one. I feel it deep within me. I need to protect both of my boys, and this is the only way to do it. I hope someday they'll understand.

I raise the pistol and take aim.

"It's never safe to make a bet like that, Bobby-doodle," I say softly, speaking to the back of his head. "I love you."

I have four bullets.

If my aim is good, I'll only need two.

Chapter 36: Ricky, New Year's Eve

It's cold, not the way people up north define cold, but cold nevertheless. That's a pet peeve of mine. Complain about the cold and someone from Boston or Chicago or some other cold place will say, "You think it's cold there? It's ten below here!" I always want to say, "Yeah but it's *supposed* to be cold there. I'm in Florida. It's *not* supposed to be cold *here*." But I never say that. Instead, I smile and agree that I'm a whiner and a wimp because I expect it to be warm where it's supposed to be warm. I am, forever and always, my mother's easygoing child, a people pleaser who sits in the shadows and asks for nothing.

Do I sound bitter? Maybe I am.

Von heard the shots, so she was the one who found them. I don't think Mom would have wanted it that way; in fact, I know she *wouldn't* have, but that's the way it was. Once you're dead, you don't have much say in such things, something the suicidal often don't seem to grasp.

Bobby had one gunshot wound to the back of his

head. Shoved into his pants—*my* pants, actually—was a moneybag from the nursery full of money, keys, my birth certificate, and the missing contents of my wallet.

Mom had one gunshot wound to the side of her head, entering at her temple. At her feet was an old .38. Shoved into her front pocket was a note to me. What it said is private, something I'll never share. Suffice it to say I've always known my mother loved me, even if she didn't show it in the most conventional sort of way. What she did wasn't necessary, but I understand she felt she didn't have a choice. She needed to protect me, but she couldn't hurt one of her sons and survive, so she chose to go with him.

No do-overs, Ricky! You lose!

Bobby had always demanded my mother's time and attention. Nothing about that had changed, regardless of what my mother's intentions were. He still had her. I still didn't.

I step harder on the accelerator, passing an old man in a beat-up Ford ranger. I'm on my way to Martha's house to celebrate New Year's Eve. I'm sure none of us feels like celebrating, but I also know we're all grateful to leave the old year behind.

Von and Ben sold the nursery shortly after my mother died. Even now, I'm unable to say *how* she died, just that she did. At any rate, the nursery was too much for Von to run without my mother, especially given what Ben was going through, and she had no interest in interviewing and hiring staff. The nursery had lost its joy for her, so she sold it to Ted. I don't know the specifics of the sale, but I know they gave him a hell of a deal. He'd been a loyal employee for many years, for all of my life, and a couple of years before. Plus, both Von and Ben felt terrible about what had happened to him, even though he repeatedly insisted it was his own fault for going to make the deposit alone. But guilt is a powerful motivator; it makes people do crazy things.

They also sold the duplex. Von couldn't live there with the sight of my mother's last moments haunting her, and as with the nursery, she had no interest in interviewing prospective tenants. No one could fill my mother's shoes. I wasn't sorry to see the duplex go. I spent my childhood wanting to live anywhere else. I certainly don't miss it now.

They moved into a retirement community outside of Tampa, just a couple of miles from Martha. On Uncle Ben's good days, which are fewer and further between, he walks the grounds and prunes the hedges. The nurses are incredibly patient, humoring him when they can. Aunt Von has filled their spacious apartment with ferns and flowers, the first time in my memory she's had any interest in plants outside the nursery. I suppose now that plants don't signify work, her love for them has expanded. Or maybe she just needs them in order to remember who she was, who we all were. I can understand that.

I think in some ways, they're happy. I know they're still in love, and I know they enjoy being close to Martha and the kids. But the loss of my mother left a hole not only in my life, but in theirs. We work hard, the three of us, to try to ease the pain, each for the other.

A fine mist begins to fall, and I turn on the wipers and set the heat to defrost. I hate the cold, especially when it's damp. I switch on my headlights and settle in for a long drive. I've made the trip to Martha's house so many times over the past few months I could do it with my eyes closed. Ty is gone for good, the divorce finalized back in August. He'd moved to California with someone nearly half his age as soon as the papers were signed, leaving behind what I considered to be the perfect family. I do my best to spend time with the kids, Justin and Monique. It's tough growing up without a father. This is something I know well. Uncle Ben filled the gap in my life, and I do my best to fill it for Martha's kids, Uncle Ben's grandkids.

I know Martha appreciates my efforts, and I know she enjoys my company. I think she hovers somewhere between appreciating me as an old friend, and appreciating me as a man. I've loved Martha as far back as I can remember. I can wait forever if that's what it takes. There is no one else for me.

As for me, I left *Swamplands*, not that Sunday evening as I'd planned, but that Sunday morning before I ever went in, as soon as I got the call from Aunt Von. Or at least as soon as I could make out what she was saying. She was understandably hysterical, as was I, when I could finally comprehend her words. I never called Andy, never cleaned out my desk, never collected my last paycheck. I just quit.

I wonder sometimes if my mother would be alive were it not for *Swamplands*. Although she never read Gerry's article, I know she was deeply troubled by what he'd found. Uncovering those old files was akin to opening old wounds. I can't help but believe it contributed to her final acts of desperation. On sleepless nights, of which there are many, I entertain fantasies of *Swamplands'* demise. Maybe Andy will get sued and have to file for bankruptcy, or maybe someone who's been ripped apart within its pages will go berserk and set fire to its offices. But I'm smart enough to know that's not how things work. More likely, given our insatiable appetite for gossip and destruction, *Swamplands* will continue to grow its audience, and Andy will continue to grow richer.

I don't see much of a future for me in my chosen profession. Things have changed. I no longer have the stomach for clickbait titles and poorly researched "facts," and I absolutely loathe online comment sections with all the anonymous ugliness they engender. For now, I make ends meet through a variety of contract jobs, everything from writing keyword-packed ad copy to ghostwriting blog posts. It isn't much, but I don't need much. My mother left me a small nest egg, squirreled away over the years since I left home. So far, I haven't had to touch it, but it's there if I need it.

So this is where we are, all of us pressing forward, searching for whatever happiness we can find. I loved my mother, and I'm sure as the years pass by I'll become less angry with her, but for now I take it day by day, moment by moment, just as she did with her recovery.

I know my mother loved me, too, even though it was in the most unconventional of ways.

I only wish she'd known that was enough for me.

Book Club Discussion Questions

1. Tabby's mother was an abused child, as was Tabby. What do you think about this dynamic? Is it common for abused children to grow up to be abusers? If so, why might this be?

2. Ricky says repeatedly that although his mother didn't always show love in a conventional way, he knows she loved him. What does he mean by this? Is unconventional maternal love as powerful as conventional maternal love? Was it for Ricky?

3. Von has learned to distance herself from Ben when he attempts intimacy. What are her reasons for this? Is it wrong to manipulate Ben, as Tabby states she must do? Why or why not?

4. Tabby acknowledges that many times throughout Ricky's childhood she put him last in her constant grief for, and search for, Bobby. Is this an understandable reaction for a grieving parent? How might it have harmed Ricky?

5. When Bobby first returns home and embraces her, Tabby feels awkward, as if she were "… hugging an unexpected guest much too closely." Why do you think that might have been the case? Can you identify with how Tabby felt?

6. Tabby initially refused to believe Bobby could be guilty of killing someone in any circumstance other than self-defense. Was this a realistic stance for her to take, given the information she had?

7. When Tabby removed her pistol from the lockbox and included it in the guns she was to return to Ben, she said she had no idea why she had done that. Do you believe her? Why might she have felt compelled to remove her pistol from the house?

8. When Tabby learned Bobby's history and sat waiting for him at the kitchen table, do you think the plan she had is the one that unfolded? Did things turn out the way you expected?

9. Ricky states he knows his mother would not have wanted Von to be the one to find her body. He then says, "Once you're dead, you don't have much say in such things, something the suicidal often don't seem to grasp." What do you think he meant by this? Was he right?

10. Ricky also says, "I know as the years pass I'll be less angry with my mother, but for now I take it day by day, moment by moment, just as she did with her recovery." Do you understand his anger? Is it justified?

More Books by Melinda Clayton

Appalachian Justice, Cedar Hollow Series, Book 1

Return to Crutcher Mountain, Cedar Hollow Series, Book 2

Entangled Thorns, Cedar Hollow Series, Book 3

Shadow Days, Cedar Hollow Series, Book 4

Blessed Are the Wholly Broken, Tennessee Delta Series, Book 1

A Woman Misunderstood, Tennessee Delta Series, Book 2

Child of Sorrow, Tennessee Delta Series, Book 3

About The Author

Melinda Clayton is the author of *Appalachian Justice*, *Return to Crutcher Mountain*, *Entangled Thorns*, *Shadow Days*, and *Blessed Are the Wholly Broken*. Melinda has published numerous articles and short stories in various print and online magazines. In addition to writing, she has an Ed.D. in Education Administration and is a licensed psychotherapist (now on retired status) in the states of Florida and Colorado.

www.ingramcontent.com/pod-product-compliance
Lightning Source LLC
Chambersburg PA
CBHW072300130726
47910CB00012B/2219